FOUR GRAVES WEST

Center Point
Large Print

FOUR GRAVES WEST

James Kane

CENTER POINT PUBLISHING
THORNDIKE, MAINE

This Center Point Large Print edition
is published in the year 2011 by arrangement with
Golden West Literary Agency.

The text of this Large Print edition is unabridged.
In other aspects, this book may vary
from the original edition.
Printed in the United States of America
on permanent paper.
Set in 16-point Times New Roman type.

ISBN: 978-1-61173-046-3

Library of Congress Cataloging-in-Publication Data

Kane, James, 1913–1983.
Four graves west / James Kane. — Center Point large print ed.
p. cm.
ISBN 978-1-61173-046-3 (lib. bdg. : alk. paper)
1. Outlaws—Fiction. 2. Police—Fiction. 3. Frontier and pioneer life—Fiction.
4. Large type books. I. Title.
PS3505.O6646F68 2011
813′.54—dc22

2010052738

I

BEN ROLLINS rolled to one side and clamped a palm over the alarm clock, smothering its raucous buzzing. He felt the woman stir against him, knew she was alert and turned to her.

"Sorry, Ben," she murmured. "But I couldn't sleep now—"

He patted her gently, got out of bed and started to dress. She stirred again, raising her head.

"I'll make coffee—" she said sleepily, but Ben leaned over and kissed her mouth, stilling her. Her lips felt warm and soft.

"I'll get coffee later," he told her. "This is no time for you to get up—four o'clock in the morning."

He stood in the darkness and turned up the bedside lamp, which cast a small glow in the bedroom.

"You sure you have to be there early?" Sue asked.

Ben nodded. "It's a five-hour ride to Telligo."

She sat up in bed. Her hair was honey blonde and loose on her shoulders, over her nightgown. Susan Rollins was twenty-two, and at seventeen she had been married to a boy not much older than herself. . . . He had been killed in the war, and she had not been in a hurry to marry again.

But Ben Rollins had been able to persuade her to wed him and build a new future with him.

Ben had put on his shirt and pants and was

buckling his gunbelt around his flat waist. He was a rangy man, hard-muscled and lean, with a small white scar over his left eye. He was twenty-seven years old.

"I said I'd try to spend more time with you," he said, grinning, "as soon as this Telligo thing is settled. But I warn you, Sue—you won't have it so easy. You'll have to quit your job in the bank, take care of the kids. And there'll be times when you'll have to get up this early in the morning to make my breakfast. . . ."

She smiled as she watched him put on his coat. His badge glittered in the lamplight.

"Come here," she said. She extended her arms out to him. "I had a bad dream, I guess—I'm worried—"

"No need." His voice was gentle. "I'm picking up a prisoner, bringing him in. That's all."

Her eyes misted. "Be careful," she said.

He crossed to her side and kissed her. She clung to him. "If something happens to you, too," she whispered, "I'll die."

He held her close. "Nothing's going to happen to me. See you tonight."

He slipped away then, and she shivered slightly and hugged the bedclothes to her. She knew she would not sleep again tonight.

THE MORNING SUN stole across the desert, changing the gray drabness of the land, bringing color to the sandstone hills and flowering cactus. On the slopes the yucca stood tall, their white blossoms eye-catching. Like sentinels, they looked down over the empty land.

The four riders followed an old wagon road that wound around the low hills. They were drifting, with no particular destination in mind, toward the Mexican border. They rode in silence, eyes squinting, scanning the hills.

Old memories haunted them.

The battered remnants of a Confederate regiment moved past them, retreating toward Texas more than two hundred miles away—the walking wounded, the hollow-eyed, the stragglers. Footsore horses and beaten men, and wagons broke down and were abandoned—old ghosts now, streaming past them, voiceless in the wind. . . .

The sun climbed into the clear Arizona sky, and the morning breeze died. Heat pressed down on them, reflecting upward from the rocks, searing into the earth. They rode hunched forward in the saddle, each man wrapped in his own thoughts.

Up ahead the barely discernible ruts of an abandoned road angled off from the one they were following. They paused here to glance off across a onetime bean field to the ruins of a small ranch house in the distance. After a moment they turned toward it in silent common consent.

One side of the adobe ranch house had fallen inward, and the risers, charred and weathered a soft gray now, appeared to make a rude cross over what remained. A small wind blew fitfully across the weed-grown yard. A few tumbleweeds were wedged against what remained of a corral fence.

The four riders eyed the scene, each with his own memories.

Hank Johnson, six feet two, gaunt and savage as a wolf, wiped sweat from under his battered hat brim. He was wearing patched and threadbare Confederate cavalry uniform trousers, and the gun on his hip, an Army pistol, was one he had "liberated" from a dead Confederate officer.

He rested his forearms on his saddle and leaned forward slightly, his eyes and his voice reflecting little regret.

"Just about like we left it, eh, boys?" He ran his eyes over the ruins while tonguing his dry, cracked lips. "Shore wish that old Mexican was here now, with his jug of *vino*." Then, remembering, he winced and rubbed his stomach. "Blast them tamales! They still burn my insides, just thinking of them."

The man mounted on the tired animal beside Johnson eased out of his saddle and limped toward the house. He was a well-built man, about Johnson's age, with shaggy red hair and bright blue eyes. He looked younger and harder than Johnson. His name was Lamont Mason; the others called him Brazos. He had been born in Texas, raised on a hard-scrabble farm on that river, and had run away when he was twelve.

He sat down on a cross-timber and tugged his boot off his right foot. His socks had holes at the heels and toes, and his boots were coming apart at the seams. He poked a finger through a hole in the sole and growled: "Forget about the *vino,* Hank. I'd kill a man right now for a good pair of boots."

The rider on the other side of Johnson unhooked his canteen and took a careful swallow of water. He was older than any of them, with prematurely gray hair, but he was still under forty. He wore a gun on his hip and one in his shoulder holster, but these were kept out of sight under a long black coat. At first glance he looked like a preacher; the others called him Deacon. He had never said a prayer in his life.

He looked past Johnson, through the years; around them now Mexican voices stirred in the stillness. Shadowy faces formed in the ruins of the old ranch house—apprehensive, frightened. . . .

The old Mexican had come out of the house to greet them as they rode up, a vanguard of a beaten army. . . . His voice had been thin, hiding his fear. "Welcome, amigos."

It had been a long war, the Deacon thought, and they had been bone-tired and running. And killing had become a habit. A few more made little difference. . . .

Brazos pulled on his boot and stood up. "Never

figgered we'd be back this way again, did we?" He looked off, remembering and not liking it. "The war was lost, but that damned General Sibley had to make one more fight."

He fished in his pockets for the makings and found nothing; he spat discontentedly.

"Cripes, I don't even have the price of a sack of tobacco!" He walked back to join the others. "Thought I'd have a better deal, after the war was over. . . ."

Johnson said cynically: "What you griping about, Brazos? We got out alive, didn't we?"

"That's about all we got," Brazos snapped. He ran his gaze over his companions. "Look at us! Three years after the war, and we're still drifting, looking for a handout!"

Deacon shrugged. "We could have gone to work. There's cattle drives going north—"

"Thirty a month and beans—the trail boss yelling at you—fighting mud and dust and Lord knows what!" Brazos pounded his fist against his saddle. "Deacon, I had enough of that in the Army!"

Johnson said mildly: "Well, we can always hold up a bank or drift into Mexico. Lot of men like us down there now—"

The young rider on his left said: "I just thought of something. Ain't there a town called Spanish Wells around here?"

Johnson nodded. "Why?"

The young rider had a name, but he had been called the Kid so long he had a hard time remembering it himself. He was an orphan. He had joined the Texas Volunteers at the beginning of the war. He had lied about his age, and they gave him a bugle and, later, a rifle. He became quite proficient with both. He had learned nothing else of value in the Army.

He said: "That's where the sarge came from."

Johnson eyed him. "The sarge?" Then, hard: "You mean Ben Rollins?"

The Kid shrugged. "Heard him talk about it lots of times. He was looking forward to going back when the war ended."

Brazos snarled: "Good for him!"

Johnson was frowning. "What you thinking, Kid?"

"I thought maybe we could look him up—"

"That blasted sergeant!" Brazos spat across his saddle. "Hated him as much as I hated the officers!" He swung up into the saddle. "You look him up if you want to, Kid!"

The Deacon rubbed his jaw thoughtfully. "Wait a minute, Brazos. Maybe we're overlooking something here." He turned to the Kid. "Still got your old Army bugle, haven't you, boy?"

The Kid nodded. He resented being called a boy, although he was not yet twenty-one. He was as good as any of his companions with a gun, but he lacked the callousness of these men who had taken over as the family he had never had.

Johnson looked at the Deacon, puzzled.

Brazos said angrily: "What the devil is he going to do with his bugle?"

The Deacon smiled. "Well, I thought it might be real sociable of us if we stopped by the sarge's place and played Ben an old Army tune."

Brazos said: "You're crazy!"

Johnson grinned. He saw some humor in it, and possibly some gain.

"Why not?" he asked Brazos. "The sarge owes us something for all those odd jobs he had us do and all those stinking details." His eyes turned flinty at the memory; then he took a deep breath and put a hand on Brazos' arm, heading off the man's angry retort. "Besides, Ben might be good for a new pair of boots. . . ."

The Deacon added his bit. "Come on, Brazos. No harm in stopping by and saying hello to an old Army buddy, is there?"

Brazos looked off across the gutted ranch house. Heat devils were dancing over the alkali flats.

"All right," he said sullenly. "But I sure hate letting him see me like this." He pulled out the linings of his empty pockets.

"Oh," Johnson said cheerfully, "maybe he's as broke as we are."

II

THEY RODE into Spanish Wells just past noon. It was a mining town less than seventy miles from the Mexican Border, surrounded by a few small cattle ranches. Cupped between rocky desert hills, it was seldom disturbed by a breeze. And this day it was hot.

The town looked deserted as they rode in, but it was only the heat that was keeping people indoors. The stamp mill about a mile out of town was working, but there was no traffic on the road to it.

They rode past the sheriff's office, eying it with instinctive wariness. But no one came out to look them over. The place looked closed.

They tied up in front of the nearest bar, The Silver King, and went inside, glad to get out of the searing sunlight.

Tim Lucas, the bartender, was seated behind the bar, his eyes closed. He had a wet towel draped across his head. A few men were playing cards at a nearby table.

Johnson slapped his palm down hard on the counter, and the bartender jerked awake. He got off his stool and walked to them, sizing them up sourly as saddle tramps.

But he drew four glasses of beer as Johnson ordered and set them down in front of them. The

Kid and Brazos took theirs, moved over to the free lunch end of the counter and began to eat hungrily.

The bartender said clearly: "That'll be eighty cents."

Johnson drank his beer in one long satisfying pull. He pushed his glass back to Lucas for a refill and said pleasantly: "That's all right, barkeep. Just charge it all to a friend of ours, Ben Rollins."

The bartender placed his palm over Johnson's empty glass and edged toward the sawed-off shotgun he kept under the counter.

Johnson's smile thinned as he understood Lucas' move. He said coldly: "Ben lives here, doesn't he?"

The bartender nodded.

The Deacon brushed his coat back, let his hand rest near his gun butt.

"We're old Army friends of Ben."

The bartender changed his mind about the shotgun. "I guess it'll be all right." He didn't want trouble with these men—a few glasses of beer and some lunch wasn't worth a man's life.

He refilled Johnson's glass, and Johnson said: "What's Ben doing these days?"

"He's the sheriff," Lucas answered.

The Deacon smiled ironically. Brazos came up to join them, stuffing a pickled egg into his mouth.

"You don't say!" Johnson said, surprised. He turned to Brazos. "Looks like the sarge went and got himself a badge!"

Brazos snarled: "He would."

The Deacon cut across him to the bartender, his voice conciliatory. "Well, we'll just stop by and say hello."

One of the men at the card table, a farmer, said: "The sheriff's out of town. Won't be back until late tonight, I hear."

"Too bad," Johnson said. "We would have liked to see him."

They had a second round of beer and then went outside, pausing in the hot sun by the hitchrack. They could wait for Ben, but all at once this no longer interested them.

Brazos ran his gaze down the empty street. There was a bank on the corner of the next block: it was the most solid-looking building in town.

Brazos turned and saw that Johnson was eying the bank. He said quietly: "You thinking what I'm thinking, Hank?"

Johnson glanced at the Deacon. "Sure hate to leave with empty pockets."

They mounted and rode to the bank. The Kid stayed with the horses.

Susan Rollins was checking her cash drawer when they walked inside. There was no one else inside the business section of the bank. George Talus, the other cashier, had gone to lunch. Myron Marshall, the banker, was in his private office—Susan suspected he was catching a nap.

Johnson and the Deacon walked to the teller's

window. Brazos waited just inside the door.

Susan looked up as they came toward her and started to push the cash drawer shut.

Johnson laid the barrel of his pistol on the small shelf of the teller's window. "Just keep quiet," he told her, "and you won't get hurt."

The Deacon went around to the teller's side of the bank. He picked up a canvas sack with the bank's name stenciled across it and walked to the big safe in a corner.

He motioned to Susan. "Open it."

Susan felt the rise of panic in her throat. She said, choked: "It's open. . . ."

Deacon frowned. He tried the handle, and the door swung open. There were cash boxes inside, but they were empty. Some papers on a shelf—ledgers.

Johnson had come around to stand beside Susan. He said: "Aw, come on, ma'am—where's the money?"

She pointed to her cash drawer. "That's all there is."

Johnson scooped out the bills, the hard currency. He made a quick count, then turned to her, disappointed. "Three hundred and eleven dollars?" His voice turned ugly. "What kind of bank is this?"

Susan licked her lips. Her voice seemed to come unstuck from between them. She was desperately afraid.

"There was more money in the safe, but it went out on the morning stage. It goes to the main office in Phoenix once a month."

Johnson turned to the Deacon. "That," he said harshly, "is the kind of luck we been running into for three years now—"

The Deacon came up and tried the other cashier's drawer. He looked at Susan. "Any money in here?"

Susan hesitated, then nodded.

"Open it!"

Outside, in the lunchroom across the street, George Talus was sitting at a window table. He paused, not liking the looks of the rider and three saddled horses in front of the bank.

The waiter was just bringing him his dinner. He said: "Keep it warm for me, Harry—I'll be right back."

The Kid was using his fingernail to pry something loose from between his teeth when George crossed the street. The Kid said: "Hey, mister—I wouldn't go in there just now."

George shot him a look, then broke into a run for the door. The Kid drew his pistol, but he couldn't shoot an unarmed man in the back. He shot in the air instead.

Brazos, alerted by the shot, whirled as George came running inside. He drew and shot without thinking, his slugs slamming George back against the wall.

Susan panicked. She started to run toward Marshall's private office just as the banker, a tall, middle-aged, graying man, stepped out. He was still half asleep, but he had grabbed the pistol from his desk drawer when he had heard the shots, and he had it in his hand when he came out.

Johnson and the Deacon fired together. Susan was in the way, and she went sprawling. The banker got off one shot before they killed him.

The Deacon scooped the rest of the money from George's cash drawer. Johnson, already moving, said grimly: "Let's get out of here!"

The Kid was holding the horses as they came running out. They hit saddle, wheeled and went galloping away.

A few people, roused by the shots, came out on the street. But they just stared.

No one followed.

III

"THERE WAS nothing I could do for her," Doctor Swanson said. He was in his office, talking to Ben Rollins. "She died a few minutes ago. . . ."

He paused and ran his fingers through his rumpled hair. His face looked drawn and haggard in the lamplight.

Ben reached down and lifted the sheet from Sue's face. Her eyes were closed, but there was a sadness death had fixed on her face.

"She was conscious for a while," the doctor went on. "Kept hanging on." He drew a tired breath. "I think she was waiting for you. Then, just before she died, she said, 'Tell Ben I'm sorry.' "

The pain stabbed through Ben, deep and lasting. Gently he lowered the sheet over Sue's face.

He said in a voice that sounded strange and far away, "Handle things for me, Doc. I'll pay for the funeral and whatever other expenses are necessary."

He stumbled out of the office then and stood on the walk, staring blindly up the deserted street. The mine-scarred hills rose in dark, mute humps against the stars. It was still hot, breathless; he knew from experience it would not cool off until after midnight.

Ben had lived there most of his life; he knew everyone in Spanish Wells. He had traveled some, but by nature he was not a wanderer. For him the war had been only an interlude—he had come back to Spanish Wells with every intention of settling down.

Now he stood in the shadows outside the doctor's office, a stranger in a strange place. His gaze wandered down the street to the hotel where he had been until he had met Sue.

He had been told a posse had formed and gone after the killers, but he placed little hope in it.

He went back to the saloon and settled in a chair at a rear table, a bottle at his elbow. There were few people inside the bar—the hour was getting late—and they left him alone. Ben drank to ease the pain in his heart. Sue's still, sad face tortured him.

He went over in his thoughts what Lucas had been able to tell him about the men who had killed Sue.

Four saddle tramps who said they had known him during the war. Army buddies! Four men who had called him *Sarge!*

He tried to pluck faces out of the recent past; out of the smoke and ruin of war, the ghosts of men he had served with rose and marched. Only four finally jelled, fitted the descriptions the bartender had given him.

Hank Johnson. Brazos. The Deacon. And the Kid.

Ben finished the bottle. Whiskey numbed the

pain in his heart, but did not kill the memory of Sue. He got up and walked to the door and looked up at the stars, trying to orient himself. But he could not bring himself to go to his room.

He slept in his office, on a cot. And he slept badly.

The posse straggled back after daybreak. He sensed it had been a half-hearted pursuit, organized after the shock had worn off, and undertaken by men who had little heart for it.

James Curzon, the mine superintendent who had been in town when it happened, was apologetic. "We lost them in the breaks south of Chino Peak," he told Ben. "Looked like they were headed for Mexico." He shook his head. "Nothing more we could do. We've no authority to cross the Border. I wired the Federal authorities in Phoenix."

Ben nodded and turned away from the tired mounted men. He walked like a man in a dream, all his reflexes slowed, his emotions knotted around the dull ache in his chest.

He stayed in town for Sue's funeral. He knew the trail of her killers would be getting cold, but he had to stay, say goodbye to the woman who had consented to share his life. And a day or two, more or less, didn't seem to matter. Ben felt he had all eternity ahead of him.

Sue was buried, along with George Talus and the banker, Marshall, in the small cemetery outside of town. Ben waited until everyone else had gone. Already the harsh Arizona sun was baking the raw earth over Sue's grave.

He stood for long minutes, the sun searing the back of his neck. He was dry-eyed, empty of feeling.

Ben wanted to say something, but he couldn't find the words. His hand fumbled inside his coat pocket for the Christopher medal Sue had given him. She had wanted him to wear it—keep him safe.

He dropped it on her grave.

He walked back to the law office like a man with time on his hands. He dropped his badge on the desk, scribbled a note to explain he was resigning (he did not want to talk to anybody) and took two boxes of shells from his desk drawer. He went out, locking the door behind him.

He did not expect to come back.

TWO DAYS later Ben picked up sign of the men he was after.

The country southeast of Chino Peak was wild and, as far as Ben knew, uninhabited. For most of the year the creek beds ran dry; in summer the few scattered waterholes became mud flats, crusted and cracked under the burning sun.

Ira Shannon's shack was backed up against a rock hill, sheltered from the winds that blew off the deserts to the south. It was put together from odds and ends of lumber and adobe from which dozens of imbedded, empty whiskey bottles seemed to catch fire as the sun went down.

A trio of cottonwood trees shaded a water trough beside a hand-dug well. Coming upon it from the higher ground to the north, Ben easily would have missed the mustanger's shack had he not known of it.

He studied Shannon's place through field glasses he took from his saddle bag. He could make out Shannon's burro (Shannon prospected for gold when he was not trapping horses) and a huddle of horses in the corral, but he could not tell if among them were the ones he had been trailing.

He lowered his glasses. The trail he had picked up led this way, but he didn't believe the killers were holed up in Shannon's shack. It was too close to Spanish Wells, for one thing—and they would know someone would be after them.

Ben rode warily, his eyes scanning the shack and the areas around it. The slanting sun burned against his back; he could feel sweat trickle down his spine.

The place looked deserted. Ben wondered if they had killed Shannon. . . .

He was within fifty feet of the dwelling when Ira stepped out. The mustanger was a short, wiry man in his forties, grizzled and trap-mouthed—a man used to silence and solitude. He was holding a shotgun on Ben, but he lowered it when he recognized Rollins.

Ira sagged against the door framing. “Glad it’s you, Sheriff.”

There was a bloodstained bandage around his balding head. A hat was jammed down over it.

Ben looked around. “Where’s Rufus? Didn’t hear him barking. . . .”

“They killed him.” The hurt showed in the mustanger’s blue eyes, hard and cold and bitter. “They killed my dog, made me cook supper for them. Then they cleaned me out of grub, took four of my best horses and rode south.”

Ben dismounted. “How long?”

“Two days ago.” Shannon set his shotgun down. “You looking for them?”

Ben nodded. He walked to the corral, looked inside. The horses the killers had left behind were huddled in a group at the far end—they looked worn out, wind-broken.

Shannon joined him.

Ben said, “You need help?”

The mustanger shook his head. “I’m all right. Need some staples, that’s all. I’ll be going into town tomorrow.” He studied Ben. “My guess is they’re headed for Mexico. Yore badge ain’t gonna help you out there.”

Ben shrugged. “I’ve resigned.” He looked off, his eyes hard. “Personal matter now, Ira.”

Shannon was silent for a moment, his eyes reflective. "They kill somebody?"

Ben nodded. "You'll hear all about it in town." He didn't feel like explaining.

Shannon knuckled his jaw. "Reckon I was lucky."

Ben was staring off toward the distant hills. He closed his eyes for a moment and seemed to see them as he remembered them—Johnson, Brazos, the Deacon and the Kid. Riding into the hazy distance, laughing, dissolving. . . .

"Four of them," Shannon muttered. "Mean as they come. And mebbe a bit crazy, too. They kept talking about the war, and about playing a joke on their good old sergeant. . . ." He shook his head. "Guess the war made killers out of a lot of men. . . ."

"Yeah," Ben said shortly. "Some of them, anyway."

He motioned toward the horses in the corral. "What are they riding now?"

Shannon thought a moment. "The young feller picked out a piebald mare. Kinda flashy, but mean; walks splay-footed. The one who looks like a minister put his saddle on a big gray stallion. Not fast, but the best of the lot—he'll outlast the others in this kind of country." He paused. "The other two are riding roan mares."

Ben said: "If you were running from the law and headed south, where would you go?"

Shannon considered. "Ain't much between here and the border 'cept sand and rocks. If they kept south they'd come across a waterhole, if it ain't dried up. Then miles beyond, inside Mexico, they'd hit an old wagon road leading to a Mexican town at the base of a small mountain range. Place called San Marcos. . . ."

"Any other towns in that direction?"

"Could be. I ain't had much opportunity to find out. Been chased out twice by the Mexican *rurales.* They don't take to gringos trapping wild horses in their country."

Ben led his horse to the trough and let him drink. He refilled his canteen at the pump.

Shannon said: "Shot me a rabbit this afternoon. Got him stewing inside. Yo're welcome—"

Ben shook his head. "Thanks, anyway."

He mounted and looked down on the mustanger. "Take care of yourself, Ira."

Shannon nodded. "Ride easy, Ben."

He watched Ben wheel away and ride south, and he waited until Ben was out of sight. Then he waved, an afterthought, and said slowly, "Luck to you, Ben," and went back inside his shack.

BEN CROSSED into Mexico at sundown. The country didn't change; the dry, eroded land looked the same. Mesas shouldered the horizon, melting into low rocky hills and gullied valleys. There was the sense of space all around him, and a desolateness that seemed to reach into infinity. It was a still and silent land, yet it held a fascination for Ben, as it had for his father, who had left the swamplands of the Carolina tidewater to settle in southern Arizona.

The wind that had blown steadily during the day, hot and dry and sucking at a man's juices, died down now as the sun dipped below the ragged horizon.

A few miles beyond, Ben came upon the waterhole Shannon had mentioned. It was a coffee-colored puddle, rimmed by reeds and flanked by desert rocks.

The men he was after had stopped there. He could see their prints in the moist sand. They had stopped to rest and to eat, and then had thrown their empty cans carelessly into the waterhole.

Ben studied the hoofprints in the moist sand until he knew he would be able to pick them out from among any others. One of them had a thinning front shoe—it looked as if a nail were pulling loose.

He hunkered down at the base of some rocks and ate a strip of jerky, washing the salt taste of it down with warm water from his canteen. He had often eaten this way during the war, and it was no discomfort for him now.

The pool water darkened as the shadows stole silently across the arid land. Ben closed his eyes, but the waterhole remained in his mind's eye.

Sue's face appeared, floating on the darkening water, sadness fixed eternally on her face.

Ben stood up and leaned against the rocks, the tight knot in his chest suddenly coming apart. He began to cry—low, wracking, uncontrollable sobs. It was the first time Ben had cried in twenty years.

Finally he straightened, wiping the tears with the back of his hand. The dull pain in his chest was gone.

He looked down on the muddy waterhole, but Sue's haunting face was no longer there.

He said softly what he had been unable to say at her grave: "Goodbye, Sue."

He mounted then and rode away toward the distant, darkening hills.

IV

THE BUGLE CALL drifted across the sandy gully, a little blurred, not quite sure of itself. But it had vigor behind it, and a youthful enthusiasm that just had to be expressed.

On the other side of the gully, Brazos turned to eye the Kid, the blazoning notes of "Johnny Reb" reawakening memories. War had been hell, but it had had its moments. . . . He stood for a beat, rifle held loosely across his waist, forgetting what he had come there for. . . .

Johnson stirred at the bugle call. He had been dozing, his back against the crumbling adobe wall of the abandoned goatherd's shack, hat pulled down over his eyes. He had been dreaming of a place vaguely like home—trees and grass and a bubbling stream rushing down a wooded hillside; a woman he had called Mother and a man, his father, who seemed always tired, stooped from endless laboring in the fields. Like all dreams, this one was inaccurate. Neither his father nor his mother were quite like that. They were the exaggerated images retained from childhood. They had been dead a long time now.

He stood up, vaguely irritated at having been awakened, and yelled for the Kid to cut it out. But the Kid, eyes closed, standing on a small rise of ground beyond the hut, didn't hear him. He was lost in some reveries of his own, and he swung through a repertory of calls he had learned—Army calls and bawdy tunes—on the battered Army bugle he had managed to retain from a war that had left him little else.

Johnson turned to the Deacon, who was dealing himself poker hands from a well-thumbed deck onto a blanket spread out in front of him.

"Darned fool! What's gotten into him?"

The Deacon palmed a card from the bottom of the deck and studied it, scowling a little. He was rusty, he thought, but he knew the old skill would come back. And he knew, too, that it was time for the four of them to split up.

Johnson came to stand over him, snarling: "You, too, Deacon. What the devil's with you?"

The Deacon looked up, smiling. "Get up on the wrong side of your dream, Hank?"

Johnson waved toward the Kid. "You'd think he owned the world, the way he's playing that darned bugle!"

The Deacon shrugged. "He's twenty," he said noncommittally. "Maybe he does."

Johnson swung back to him. "One hundred sixty-three dollars, his share of the bank money. How much of the world can he own with that?"

The Deacon said, "Sit down, Hank. It's too hot to argue the merits of youth and an empty-pockets philosophy with you."

Johnson started to say something, then thought

better of it. He walked toward the goat pen where they had put up their horses and stopped on the way to pick up a hunk of adobe. He cocked his arm and threw it at the Kid a hundred feet away.

The adobe hit in front of the Kid, breaking into several pieces. The Kid lowered his bugle and looked toward Johnson, who shook his fist at him.

"I said to cut it out!" Johnson yelled.

The Kid eyed the older man for a long moment wth a cool, rebellious gaze. He was not afraid of Johnson. But he had a feeling for the man, like the feeling for a father he had never had, and he allowed Johnson this authority.

He lowered his bugle and waved acquiescence. Johnson walked on into the corral.

The Kid stared across the seemingly limitless dull plain toward the distant hills. Between them the land was cut and crisscrossed by innumerable lines of erosion. The hills seemed to float on a sea of shimmering hot air—blue, ragged, unsubstantial.

They had been there more than a day, resting. Although no one up to now had spoken of it, the Kid knew they had come to the end of something that had been formed and welded between them during the war. The bond between them had been wearing thin these past months; it had only taken something like robbing a bank to bring it to a head.

For a moment the Kid, contemplating this, felt lost. He had grown up in the company of these men—they had been his family. He was old enough, surely, to be on his own, but he did not know what he wanted to do with his life. He knew only that he did not look forward to being tied down to a job. He was restless, and there was a singing in his blood. *Out there, he thought, somewhere, anything could happen—something good as well as bad.*

He saw Brazos coming back across the gully, a blocky, powerful man, hard and impatient as always. There was a restlessness in Brazos, too, but he was mean and suspicious these days, and the Kid sensed he was growing sour with the years.

Hank was in the corral, examining the horses. He turned now and called out to Brazos, and the blocky man swung toward the corral, frowning.

Johnson lifted the left front foot of Brazos' roan off the ground, bending it at the knee so that Brazos could see the worn shoe.

"Couple of nails pulled loose," Hank said. "She'll lose the shoe any time—"

Brazos cursed. "Just my luck!" he snarled. "We all get the pick of mounts at that mustanger's place, but I'm the jasper who has to get stuck with a horse with a worn shoe!"

Johnson said angrily, "I thought you checked your horse, Brazos!"

They walked back to join the Deacon, who had put away his cards and was rolling up his blanket.

"I'm ready to move on," Johnson said. He waited a moment for the Kid to join them; then: "I'm figgerin' on moving on alone."

Brazos shrugged. "I'm figgerin' the same, Deacon."

The Deacon cracked his knuckles thoughtfully. "The war's over," he said absently. "Nothing much to hold us together any more."

He looked off into the distance.

"See anything out there, Brazos?"

Brazos shook his head.

Johnson said impatiently, "You can bet that posse quit long ago."

"I was thinking of Ben Rollins," the Deacon said.

"The sarge?" Johnson spat on the ground. "Why should he come after us? The money wasn't his."

The Deacon rubbed his hands together. It was an old habit when he was uneasy, and the gesture added to the impression (for those who did not know him) that he was a man of the cloth.

"You're not remembering Ben," he said quietly. "That was his town we hit. We killed some people in that bank."

Brazos sneered. "One man! I never liked him, Deacon. But I never figgered Ben to be a fool, either!"

Johnson made an uneasy gesture. "I don't know, Brazos. Can't ever tell about Ben. Once he got something locked in his mind—"

"Then why are we splitting up?" the Kid broke in. "Four of us against Ben are pretty good odds."

"I guess it's just come time, that's all, Kid." The Deacon looked at Brazos. "We'll take our chances with Ben, then?"

"Fine with me," Brazos said coldly. He looked at Johnson. "I was thinking of heading for Tampico myself, to sign up on some ship." His eyes lighted up with some inner fantasy. "Always wanted to sail on something bigger than a river."

"I been thinking of joining up with Major Sutter," Johnson said. "Heard he and some of the boys from the Fifth Cav refused to surrender after Lee quit. They took over some Mexican town just below the border, southeast of here."

"That son-of-a-bitch!" Brazos spat. "Well, I wish you luck, Hank. Me, I've had enough of the Army!"

He walked to his horse, gave it a kick out of pure spite, and started to saddle up.

Johnson eyed the Deacon. "Where you headed?"

"Haven't thought much about it," the Deacon confessed. "Maybe the California gold fields."

Johnson shrugged. "Never cared for pick-and-shovel work myself." He started to walk off. The Kid followed him.

"Mind if I ride along, Hank? I'm kinda hankering to see some of the old bunch myself. . . ."

Johnson hesitated, then nodded.

They saddled up, filled canteens, split the remaining tins of food among them.

Johnson and the Kid were the first to mount. Johnson looked down at Brazos, who was checking the cinch strap on his mount. They had been together a long time; now he said simply: "See you sometime, Brazos."

Brazos waved casually.

Johnson and the Kid rode away from the hut, heading southeast.

The Deacon came up as Brazos mounted. "We passed an old road on the way in," he said. "Seemed to be heading for those mountains." He paused. "Might be a town up ahead—maybe a blacksmith—"

Brazos nodded. "I'll give it a try."

He grinned, a wide and reckless grin. "I'll think about you, Deacon, when I snuggle up to some dark-haired *señorita in Tampico*."

The Deacon smiled. "Do that," he said.

He watched Brazos ride off. Brazos wouldn't make it to Tampico. His horse would go lame in less than five miles. But that was Brazos' hard luck.

He took a long thin cigar (he had been hoarding them) from his inside pocket and lighted up. He took his time. He had told his companions he would be heading for the California gold fields, just in case Ben caught up with any one of them and forced information out of him. The Deacon's plans were to head for the New Mexican border town of San Paulito, then go, in easy stages, to El Paso. From there he would ride wherever the winds blew. . . .

He mounted when the sun was low over the far hills and the fierce heat of the day receding. He rode at a leisurely pace, conserving the big gray's strength. The Deacon was a gambler, but he never played the odds against his life.

He followed in Brazos' tracks for several miles; then, along a rocky stretch of ground which would leave no sign of his passage, he turned northeast toward San Paulito.

V

BEN ROLLINS rode up to the goatherd's shack early the next morning. He slouched tiredly in the saddle as he made a quick survey of the place.

Someone, he thought with mild interest, had built this shelter, dug a shallow well in the arroyo that ran behind it and found water. He had erected a canopy of tough manzanita branches to shade his burro and a stone corral to pen his goats. Someone had lived there for a time and then gone away—the Sonoran desert was dotted with abandoned huts.

The men he was after had been there. The freshly opened cans from which they had eaten were drawing morning flies and desert ants, and from inside one a small gray lizard poked his head out to look at the rider.

Ben dismounted and walked to the corral. They had rested there for some time, he thought, noting the horse dung inside, and this gave him a bleak sense of satisfaction.

He studied the hoofprints leading away from the corral for a moment and then went back to his mount for his canteen. He carried it down into the gully, filling it from the shallow, muddy well.

Mounting, he studied the tracks leading away from the corral. He saw where two men had ridden off first, toward the southeast, and he noted that the Kid's splay-footed piebald was one of these.

The other two headed directly south, toward the distant hills. One was the Deacon's big gray—the other had a loose shoe. Ben had not expected his quarry to split up. It would take longer to track them down—but he had the time.

He suspected that the rider mounted on the horse with the bad shoe was Brazos, and looking off toward the horizon, he knew that by this time Brazos would be in trouble. It did not surpise him. Brazos had never been one to take care of his mount, no matter how much the necessity had been drilled into him. To Brazos, a horse was just something he rode.

Ben's thoughts went back to Brazos' Army file:

Born Lamont Mason, Brazos County, Texas, April 12, 1838. Parents, farmers. Two sisters, one brother, died in infancy. Enlisted Fort Sam Houston. Unquestioned loyalty to the Confederacy, expert rifleman. Indifferent soldier. Promoted to corporal during battle at Mills Church; demoted two days later for striking an officer. Suspended court-martial sentence.

This was what the Army had on Brazos, but Ben remembered other things about the man. A mean temper, impatience, personal slovenliness. A man of unbridled passions, he had been charged with the rape of a woman on a small farm—but this was during the last desperate days of the war and the Army had ignored it.

• • •

BEN FOLLOWED the tracks away from the goat-herd's shack. A few miles south they crossed a stretch of *malpais,* and here Ben picked up a worn horseshoe. He looked toward the hills again. Brazos would be afoot; he could be just about making the town Shannon had told him about—San Marcos.

Ben tossed the shoe aside and rode on across the stretch of hardpan until he came upon a little used wagon road that came angling up from the southwest. He pulled up, studying the prints in the softer sand.

One man afoot, leading a limping horse. That would be Brazos. There was no sign of the Deacon's big gray.

Ben turned to look back toward the goatherd's shack, lost on the desolate plain. He guessed that somewhere along the stretch of hardpan, the Deacon had cut away, leaving no tracks.

Of the four men he was after, Ben knew this man least of all. He had never liked the Deacon, but the Deacon had given him the least trouble. A quiet, withdrawn sort of man, cool in times of battle, he appeared to find most things humorous—but his was an inside, black humor which he shared with no one.

Ben's gaze reached into the distance. The Deacon could be headed anywhere, but Brazos would be the easier to find.

He turned his horse south, toward San Marcos.

VI

SAN MARCOS was one of a chain of villages founded more than a century ago by Father Kino; the outflung Spanish empire that followed Coronado, founded by the Cross and held by the Sword against the marauding Apaches and the fierce Yaquis. Then, as the empire shrank and faded, the village had fallen into decay; the mission church, built by the aching backs and calloused hands of converted natives, was no longer in use except when, once a month, a young, hardy Franciscan monk out of Santa Lucia rode a burro fifty miles to receive confession and to hold mass.

Goats and their by-products were the town's main industry. Hand-woven baskets and some pottery was sold and traded. But for the most part the people of San Marcos were isolated and self-contained.

It had been a long time since strangers had come to San Marcos.

The woman who ran the combination store and cantina across the plaza from the church thought of this as she pressed stiffly against the small counter and watched the *Americano* sprawled in a chair by one of the three plank tables. He was laughing deep in his throat as he watched fifteen-year-old Carmelita dart about, scooping up the small change he tossed on the floor.

Rosa was fat and shapeless now, and her broad, stolid features showed there was more Indian than Spanish in her blood. There was an old shotgun within reach, under the counter; but she sensed this man would kill her as easily and indifferently as she killed a fly.

Her husband had gone to Santa Lucia on his weekly trip—she knew the few men in the village would not interfere.

"Carmelita!" she called sharply.

The girl paused, lifting her eyes to her mother. She was flushed with excitement, her small breasts heaving against the cheap cloth of her blouse.

"Come here!" Rosa ordered sharply.

Carmelita hesitated.

"He is a beast," her mother warned. "He will harm you!"

A flash of fear crossed the young girl's face, and she started to back away toward the counter.

Brazos reached out and caught her by the arm. He looked at Rosa, a hard light in his eyes.

"What'd you tell her?"

The older woman eyed him with impassive gaze. "I told her to come and help me here—"

"Yo're a liar!" Brazos sneered. "I savvy just enough Mexican lingo to know what you told her."

He pulled Carmelita roughly to him, across his lap. "I ain't had a woman in a long time—"

He slid his free hand down to his holstered gun as Rosa made a move for the under-the-bar shotgun. *"Easy!"* he warned. He stood up, still holding the terrified young girl by the wrist; his right hand remained on the butt of his Colt.

"Straighten up and come away from there!" he told Rosa.

Fear made a crack in the older woman's stolidity. She backed away from the gun, pausing at the corner of the counter.

"She is only a girl," she said. Her voice was low, choking in her throat. "There are others in San Marcos—perhaps more willing—"

She paused, her eyes darting toward the doorway as the bells of the old mission began to ring. They shattered the midday stillness, clanging loudly.

Brazos' eyes narrowed. "What's that for?"

Rosa shook her head. "Sebastiani. He always rings the bells when the priest from Santa Lucia comes to San Marcos. But—" She stopped talking, her eyes sliding to him, a question in them.

Brazos scowled. "They were ringing when I rode in," he said.

"Yes," the woman answered. "He is an old man, Sebastiani. He also rings the bells when a stranger comes to San Marcos."

Brazos' smile thinned on his lips. "The bells are ringing, but it is not time for the padre from Santa Lucia, is it?"

Rosa shook her head.

Brazos pushed Carmelita away from him; the girl ran quickly to her mother's side.

Slowly Brazos drew his Colt. Rosa pushed the girl behind her; fear showed deep down in her black eyes.

"Reckon the Deacon was right," Brazos murmured, eying the open doorway. "He knew the sarge better than all of us."

He flipped the cylinder out, checked the loads in the chambers and slipped the gun back inside his holster.

"Don't go away," he told them. There was a smile of bravado on his lips as he headed for the door. "I'll be right back."

THE HOT SUN beat down on the ancient adobes flanking the village square. The sound of the bells stopped as Brazos paused by the communal well. The echoes beat back and forth in the narrow alleys and then faded into the stillness.

Brazos waited by the well. With the dying of the bells he heard a horse walking, the sound of its shod hoofs against the old cobblestones magnified by the adobe walls flanking the narrow street. He looked across the plaza, but he could not tell from which alley the sound came. And then, abruptly, the horse stopped. And the sense of danger in the sudden silence was more intense because of it.

He crossed quickly to the open-fronted

blacksmith shop where his horse stood, tied to a support. The blacksmith was firing up coals in the pit. He turned as Brazos said quickly:

"How long, Chico?"

The man lifted a seamed, brown face from the forge and eyed Brazos. His name was not Chico, and he did not understand English.

Brazos made a quick gesture, indicating he wanted to ride; the Mexican blacksmith nodded. Brazos kept glancing across the plaza. It was very quiet now in the village, yet he could not hear the unseen rider.

His smile was forced.

The blacksmith picked up the animal's foot to show Brazos he had put on a new shoe; then he smiled and held out his hand.

"Dos pesos," he said.

Brazos took out a silver dollar and gave it to the man, who nodded gratefully.

Brazos led his animal away from the blacksmith shop, pausing by the church steps. He waited there, drawing his rifle from his saddle scabbard. His eyes probed the several narrow streets that debouched into the plaza.

The silence hung dangerously on the afternoon heat.

"Ben!" he called out harshly. "I know it's you!"

The silence rang with his voice, then settled back into stillness.

Brazos licked his lips. Maybe it wasn't Ben.

Maybe it was someone else—a villager returning home. Maybe he was just jumpy.

He thought of the girl in the cantina, but a vague fear made him change his mind. *It was best,* he thought uneasily, *that he leave San Marcos.*

He turned to mount his horse, and in that instant he felt a prickle at the back of his neck, a sudden sharp warning, although he heard nothing. He whirled quickly to look across the plaza.

Ben Rollins walked into view, emerging from one of the narrow alley-streets that led into the village square.

Brazos watched him, feeling a measure of security with the rifle in his hands. The man, he thought sourly, didn't seem the same without a uniform, the sergeant's stripes on his sleeve. He didn't loom as large or radiate the same hard authority. Just another man with a gun on his hip—

Brazos said quite calmly: "It's been a long time, Sarge." Then, as Ben made no reply, he added with mock surprise: "What are you doing way down here?"

Ben kept moving slowly toward him, watching Brazos. "Looking for you," he said. His voice held no emotion.

Brazos set himself for what he knew was coming. His white teeth flashed in a grin that lighted up his tough, reckless face.

"Cripes," he said, "you shouldn'ta done that, Sarge. You got yoreself a nice job back in that home town of yores. No need to ride way down here." He waited, but Ben said nothing. He kept walking slowly toward Brazos, cutting the distance between them.

Brazos' voice tightened. "Sarge, what we took couldn't have broke the bank. They wouldn't have sent you after us just for that?"

Ben said nothing. He knew Brazos well enough to realize he could handle that rifle better than most men. All he wanted was to get close enough to cut down the odds. . . .

"We shot up a couple of people," Brazos admitted. "We didn't want to—but the darn fools forced it on us." He grinned wolfishly. "You know how it is, Sarge—killing gets to be a habit. . . ."

Ben said: "One of those people was a woman."

Brazos frowned. "She die?"

Ben nodded.

"That was an accident," Brazos said. "She ran in front of me—"

He paused, sensing the implacable purpose in the advancing man, knowing that words would not buy Ben off.

"Yore woman?" His voice was thin now.

Ben nodded slightly. He was close enough now, and he was tired of talking. Brazos' words meant nothing to him. There was only the heat and the stillness, and this strange plaza in a village he knew nothing about—just a place where he had to come to kill a man.

Brazos' sharp tone halted him. "That's close enough, Sarge!" The killer stood quietly now, his rifle held with deceptive carelessness across his waist. But Ben knew Brazos could whip that muzzle up and fire in a split-second.

"I'm sorry about the woman," Brazos continued, and then, almost as an afterthought, he brought his rifle up and fired in one quick, easy movement. He knew he hit Ben; he had that one flash of knowledge before he died.

Ben's bullets hit him in the chest, spinning him back. He fell across the church's lower steps, and for a few moments he seemed to be trying to climb them to the heavy, ancient doors that hung open. He was not aware of what he was doing, and after a while he went still.

Ben walked to him, holstering his gun. He could feel blood start to ooze warmly down his thigh into his boot. But in those few moments he was unaware of any pain. There was numbness in his right leg, and that was all.

He came to stand over Brazos' body, seeing not the man but a woman's sad face looking up at him from the doctor's table in Spanish Wells. A lump formed in his throat, momentarily choking him; then it passed. As he started to turn away, his right leg collapsed under him.

He went down slowly, quite surprised.

VII

TIME PASSED. No one came into the plaza to help him. On the outer edges of the silence, Ben could hear the distant cackling of chickens, the occasional baaing of goats. A dog barked once or twice. But it all seemed far away and remote; the sounds seemed to have no connection with the hot, dusty plaza in a Mexican village lost and forgotten by time.

Ben understood. Two strangers from another country had invaded the town, and one had killed the other. It was not callousness that immobilized the villagers, but fear.

After a while Ben struggled to a sitting position. He hitched himself up on the first steps of the church and then, with trembling fingers, examined the rifle wound in his thigh. The bullet had nicked the bone but had not broken it, and for this Ben was thankful.

He bound the wound as best as he could with his neckerchief, then whistled for his horse. The animal came to him from the quiet of the alley, dragging its reins. It stopped just in front of him and Ben hitched himself up on his one good leg, hanging onto the saddle horn.

He clung there for a moment, knowing he was too weak to pull himself up into the saddle. The cantina across the plaza drew his attention.

Hanging hard on his saddle horn, just lightly touching the cobbles with his wounded leg, he and his horse headed for Rosa's place.

Rosa watched him approach. When Ben was halfway across the plaza, she went back inside the store for her shotgun.

Ben paused a few feet from the cantina. The sun was hot on his back. He could feel unseen eyes watching him, pressing but not dangerous. He sighed heavily and wiped sweat from his face. He was still losing blood, but more slowly now, and he knew that the dull throbbing at the back of his head was the result of weakness.

He'd like to rest inside that cantina, in its inviting coolness—he'd like to sleep for a long while.

But the woman appeared in the doorway, her face hostile, a shotgun in her hands. Behind Rosa, Ben glimpsed the frightened face of a young girl, and he thought: *I can't blame her.*

"Tequila," he said. His mouth was dry, and he had difficulty shaping the word.

Rosa shook her head firmly.

Ben reached inside his pocket and took out a silver dollar. He held it up so she could see it. "Tequila," he repeated. Then, in the little he knew of Border Mexican: *"Por favor."*

Rosa hesitated. She turned, said something to the girl behind her.

Ben waited, hanging onto his saddle horn. He was beginning to feel very light-headed.

Then the girl appeared with the bottle of tequila. Rosa took it from her and looked at Ben. There was a distance of ten feet between them; she did not trust him. She had trusted Brazos. . . .

She motioned to Ben. "The money," she said. "Throw it inside."

Ben was surprised. "You speak American?"

"I was born in El Paso."

The answer brought up a flash of memory in this woman—a memory that seemed a thousand years old—of a slim, dark-eyed, dark-haired girl who had laughed and danced and thought the world was bright and young and beautiful. . . .

Ben said: "I'll pay five dollars for a bed, some food and a day's rest."

Rosa shook her head. She was back in San Marcos, and only the deep hurt remained.

"The money," she repeated harshly.

Ben tossed the silver dollar past her into the cantina. He heard it hit the floor and roll a bit, then stop.

The woman kept the shotgun leveled at him as she moved half the distance to Ben, placed the bottle on the ground, then retreated slowly to the doorway.

Ben smiled.

"Thanks, anyway," he said. He edged his horse close to the bottle, then took a deep breath. He knew if he let go of the saddle horn, he'd fall and wouldn't get up.

He looked at Rosa. He could feel the cold sweat on his face. His eyes blurred, and she seemed to undulate in the doorway. He gritted his teeth and, clinging with his left hand to the horn, stretched down and picked up the bottle. He waited a few moments more for his head to quit spinning. Then he pulled the cork with his teeth, held it between his fingers as he put the bottle to his mouth and took a long swallow.

The fiery liquid burned down his throat and cleared his head. He jammed the cork back and stuck the bottle inside his saddle bag. It still took a teeth-grating effort to mount.

He looked around the empty plaza.

Rosa said harshly: "That man you killed—he does not belong here."

Ben nodded. "I'll take care of it."

He rode back to where Brazos' horse waited by the body. Flies were buzzing over the congealing blood in the dead man's chest.

Ben took another swallow of tequila. It helped him step down, heave Brazos' limp body across the saddle of his horse.

Leading the dead man's horse, Ben rode out of San Marcos. The sound of his passage rang against the hot adobe walls, magnified in the stillness. . . . It was not until he was on the narrow trail out of town that he heard the mission bells ring out.

They were glad, Ben thought dryly, to see him go.

• • •

BEN MADE it all the way back to the goatherd's abandoned hut before dark. He buried Brazos in a shallow grave in an old stream bed where the sand made it easier to dig. Toward the end he was a little delirious. He paused and stared out across the darkening plain and thought he saw men getting ready to mount. They were in a thicket in an early morning ground mist, wraith figures, soundless and grim-faced. . . . It was the morning of the battle for Bent's Ford again. . . . Ben yelled at Brazos and Deacon and Johnson. . . . He saw the Kid, a slim, reckless-faced boy, raise his trumpet. . . . He yelled again and started toward them and finally sank down, exhausted, and fell asleep. . . .

The morning sun on his face awoke him. He felt terribly thirsty, but the pain in the back of his head was gone, and he felt stronger.

The bullet wound in his thigh had ceased bleeding.

His leg pained him as he walked, and he favored it by limping. He piled a few stones on Brazos' grave and stood looking down on it. Brazos had killed Susan. He had admitted it.

But avenging her did not alleviate the terrible loneliness in Ben, nor dull the urgency he felt about finding the others.

There was nothing else in his life now except this—to run down the Deacon, Johnson and the Kid.

He tied Brazos' horse to his cantle and rode away.

BEN RETRACED his steps to the stretch of hardpan where he had lost the Deacon. He had a choice: He could go after the tall, dour man who was probably the most dangerous member of his quarry, or he could set out after Johnson and the Kid. The thought came to him, as he studied the distant, desolate hills, that if he went after the Kid and Johnson he would lose the Deacon.

Find the Deacon, he reflected, and he would know where Johnson was headed.

But the Deacon could have gone anywhere from here—southeast toward Vera Cruz or Tampico, or, doubling back, west toward California.

A faint memory of a conversation nagged at Ben now—memory of an evening around a bivouac fire when Johnson had asked the Deacon if he had ever married.

The Deacon had evaded the question. He was a cold man, not easily reached. Yet a flash of something had lightened his gaze, and Brazos, seeing it, had pressed the subject with his characteristic tactlessness. *Sure, women aren't the Deacon's dish. Cards, sure. Gambling, of course. But women!*

Just that once the Deacon had shown emotion, revealed the crack in his armor.

There had been a woman once. He had never

married her. But she meant something to him—something special. Some day he might even go back to see her at a small ranch in west Texas, just outside a town called West Bend.

It was a long chance—a flash of memory in the midst of war. He could be wrong.

But Ben decided to go with it. He rode parallel to the hardpan for miles, heading eastward as well as the terrain allowed. The land remained barren, the hills jagged and desolate except for an occasional turkey buzzard or low-skimming hawk.

Once, in the far distance, he saw a village. But he gambled that the Deacon had not gone that way—and five miles beyond he was proven right.

The tracks of the Deacon's big gray showed up in a sandy wash; they headed back for the border in a straight line.

Ben followed him.

The Deacon was not expecting pursuit, but he was moving fast. Ben came upon his campfires, few and far between. There had been more than a day's distance between them, and even though Ben drove himself, making only the necessary stops to rest both animals, he gained very little on the man he was after.

He crossed back into the United States in New Mexico and followed the Deacon toward Texas. He saw little evidence of the war that had almost torn the country apart, that in one way or another had altered the lives of everyone.

Here and there he came upon small deserted ranch houses, abandoned for whatever reason in the wake of war—the menfolk killed or maimed or just tired of it all.

He ran across hundreds of half wild cattle; lean-flanked, long horns sharpened to knife point, they had survived and even multiplied.

Most of them were unbranded, born during the war years when no one had the time to take care of them. But Ben knew that men were getting rich (or hanged) branding mavericks on the Texas and New Mexican plains. A whole new era was opening up as the rails pushed eastward toward the Kansas plains. . . .

He knew this, but it did not touch him. What went on in the country no longer concerned him; ambition had died with the woman on Doctor Swanson's operating table.

He crossed into Texas and found there was a West Bend. He lost the Deacon's tracks, but it did not bother him. He knew where the Deacon was headed.

The town was up close to the mountains, high enough to escape the heat of the lowlands. It was raining when Ben rode in.

He left his horses at the stables, got himself a bath and a shave, and lingered over the first warm, decent meal since he had left Spanish Wells.

He knew the Deacon was there somewhere.

He bought some canned goods, tobacco and coffee at the general store, which was run by a one-armed man by the name of Fred Garvey.

He tried to remember the Deacon's Army file:

Joshua Frost, born March 15, 1830, Richmond, Virginia. Parents: Frank and Ellie Frost, sharecroppers. . . .

That was about all Ben remembered; he knew there had not been much more. What the Deacon had been, had done, had become, before he joined the Army had not been revealed in his records. . . .

"Sure," the storekeeper said as he filled Ben's order. "Joshua Frost was in here last night. Been five years since I last saw him. War didn't change him much."

He paused, eyed Ben.

"You a friend of his?"

"We were in the same company."

Garvey frowned. "Never was much for the war; never solves anything. Never was for slavery, either. But the way them Northern carpetbaggers are taking over—"

Ben cut him off. "The Deacon used to talk about a ranch he wanted to come back to, someplace around here."

"Deacon?"

Ben smiled. "Some of the boys used to call him that—guess it kinda stuck with me, too."

Garvey scratched his head. “Yeah—know what you mean.” He turned away from Ben to look off. “Lucy Barnes’ place. ’Bout seven miles out, on the old Henderson road. Can’t miss it. Ain’t nothing else out that way for twenty miles.”

Ben picked up his supplies. He was at the door when Garvey said: “Guess Joshua’ll be surprised to see you.”

Ben paused. “Yeah—reckon he will.”

VIII

LUCILLE BARNES stood by the window of the small ranch house, watching the rain sift across the face of the gray-weathered barn. On the table behind her three candles flickered on the cake she had made last night when she was happier, and the thought of being thirty and alone and having nothing to look forward to had been forgotten in the joy of seeing a man she had thought dead ride back into her life.

She had been plain as a girl, but maturity had made her attractive; she had a fine figure. But age was beginning to show—it had been a long time since there had been any glow to her life.

There was a fire in the wood stove, but the warmth did not reach her. Her gaze was on the empty road that wound toward the distant, rain-obscured hills.

The Deacon fingered his whiskey glass as he eyed the woman. He was not much of a drinker, and he had planned on champagne. But there was none to be had in West Bend, and he had settled for this. . . .

"It's a fine cake," he said at last. "And thirty is a fine age for a woman. She's got the worst of life behind her and, as the poet said, the best is yet to come."

He tried to make his voice light, but it did not

come out that way. He was a cold man, and even his attempts at sentiment did not ring true.

She turned to look at him. There were dark circles under her eyes. "A man said that—not a woman." Her smile was sad. "I thought you were dead."

He shrugged and sipped his whiskey.

"You never wrote—not once."

"It was the war," he said, trying to dismiss it.

"Other men wrote to their wives. . . ."

"Wives?"

She paused, and shame burned in her cheeks. She turned back to the window, hiding her thoughts from him. The rain touched the windowpanes and made crooked runnels down to the sill.

"You're right," she said, her voice barely audible. "I have no hold on you."

He got up and went to her. He stood behind her for a moment, not speaking, feeling sorry for the woman. It had been an impulse, coming here, born out of loneliness and an old memory, magnified by time into something he did not really want. He regretted coming back now.

"We're friends," he said finally, "old friends." He put his hand on her shoulder, pulling her gently around to face him. "Let's celebrate your birthday—and my return."

Her eyes searched his, looking for something she did not find, something she knew now she'd never see there. She nodded, her voice listless.

"Why not?"

He kissed her on the neck, his hand reaching around her waist. She stood very still, not responding, and after a moment he let her go. They walked back to the table together.

"Where's the kid?" His voice was brusque.

"Johnny?"

"He was two years old when I knew him," the Deacon said. "Sickly, if I remember."

"He's dead," she said. "Rheumatic heart, the doctor told me. He never really had a chance at life."

"Like his father, eh?" The Deacon watched her cut a slice of cake, place it on a dish and push it to him.

"Like his father," Lucy repeated. She had cried over both, but it was long over now, and she no longer cried. She had been a widow when the Deacon had come into her life, and a boy to raise. Now she had nothing.

The Deacon reached out and poured a generous amount of whiskey into her glass. He eyed her, smiling, hiding what he felt from her. He'd be riding in the morning.

She stood over the cake, trying to muster up some feeling of gaiety, even if forced. She was not very good at it. She shivered.

"Go ahead," he urged. "It'll warm you up a bit."

She raised the glass to her lips. *Why not?* she

thought. Thirty is a bad time for a woman. Forty is worse, but it's still ahead. Maybe whiskey will make it all easier to take. . . .

The first swallow gagged her.

The Deacon said sympathetically: "Maybe you'd better mix it with water."

She nodded, tears in the corners of her eyes. She walked to the kitchen pump with the glass, and something moving outside caught her attention.

She paused at the pump, then went to the window.

There was a rider out on the road, a shapeless figure in a poncho and pulled-down hat. He was trailing a riderless horse behind him. . . .

THE DEACON watched her for a moment, picking at his cake. Then, frowning: "What's wrong, Lucy?"

"A rider," she said. "He's coming here."

She was mystified. It was a bad day for anyone to be out, and her ranch was a long way from town. She was not expecting anyone.

The Deacon surged to his feet and crossed quickly to her, hiding the sudden uneasiness in his eyes. He looked out to the distant road. He could not recognize the rider, and the horse trailing behind was a roan, not unlike a hundred others. But something about the rider, the way he rode, revived memories of nights long past under rain-laden clouds when a man's hard voice had roused him and others like him. “Mount up! We’re moving out!”

A voice of command, from out of the war years. . . .

He stepped back, his hand dropping to the gun hidden under his long coat.

Lucy turned. What she saw in his face frightened her.

“That man,” she said, “you know him, Joshua?”

He kept his eyes on the approaching rider. “Maybe,” he answered. His voice was flat now, unresponsive.

“Who is he?”

“Not a friend,” he said. He thought he had thrown Ben off his trail, but he was not really surprised. Deep down, he had always known Ben would show up.

He stepped back from the window, pulling the woman with him.

“Go into the bedroom,” he told her. “Stay there.”

She didn’t move. Fear held her motionless—fear for this man she loved, however hopelessly.

“Joshua—maybe he isn’t—”

He pushed her gently in the direction of the bedroom. “It’s Ben,” he said, convinced. “My old Army sergeant—”

“But why?” Lucy’s voice was bewildered as well as frightened. “Why would he—?”

Outside, the rider stopped. There was, for a moment or two, only the whisper and patter of rain across the roof and against the window. Then Ben's voice came, loud and clear:

"Deacon!"

Lucille stared at Joshua. *Deacon?*

"I guess you know why I'm here," Ben said. His voice was impatient.

"I'll send him away," Lucille said. She could think of nothing else to do; she knew she could not hide in the bedroom. This was, after all, her house.

The Deacon tried to stop her, but she twisted away from his grasp. She went to the door and opened it just enough to see the man who stood outside.

Ben had taken off his poncho, draping it across the saddle of his horse waiting in the yard. He stood a few feet from her in the slanting rain, and she saw a big man with grim wet features and a gun thonged down on his thigh. His features softened as he saw her, and he seemed sorry she was there.

"They told me in town," he said. "They said he'd be here—"

"They were mistaken," she interrupted harshly. "There's no one here by that name!"

Behind her the Deacon said coldly: "Let him in, Lucy. He's coming in anyway. . . ."

Lucy shivered. "No. This is my house. I won't—"

Ben walked toward her. "I'm sorry, ma'am," he said. "I didn't want it this way."

He pushed her aside gently as he stepped in the house. He saw the Deacon by the stove as his gun came up, but he was not surprised. He moved violently, spilling away from the woman and firing at the same time. He saw the Deacon stagger and go down to one knee. Ben started to fire again, but the woman stepped in front of him, grabbing at his gun hand.

"No, no. My God, no!"

Ben tried to shake her loose. He was as much afraid for her as for himself. But the Deacon was slumping over, falling, the gun slipping from his hand. . . .

Lucille turned and ran to him. She pillowed the Deacon's head in her lap, the tears flowing freely. "Joshua, Joshua."

Ben walked to them, holstering his gun. The Deacon was alive, but he felt drained now, no longer cared.

"Ben—" The Deacon's voice was a whisper.

Ben knelt beside the woman. He saw now where one of his bullets had shattered the Deacon's right elbow. He had seen wounds like that in the war, and he knew that even if the man lived, he'd never be a whole man again.

"Knew you'd come, Ben."

Ben said quietly: "Where's Hank—and the Kid?"

"Headed south. . . . Planning to join up with Major Sutter. Remember him—the major?"

Ben nodded, his eyes hard.

"Took over some Mexican town south of El Paso. Major Sutter—maybe a company of bitter men—like him."

Ben straightened.

The Deacon's pained eyes followed him. "Why, Ben?" Then, as Ben looked down on him, "Why all this? That bank we robbed—your home town, I know. But why?"

"Three dead people," Ben said coldly. "One of them was a woman—"

Understanding came into the Deacon's gaze. "Your . . . wife?"

Ben nodded.

The Deacon's eyes closed. "Damn Brazos," he said bitterly. "He—"

"He's dead," Ben cut in grimly.

He looked at the woman. There was nothing he could say to her that would help; nor was he inclined to speak.

He left the house, closing the door firmly behind him. Lucy heard him ride away a few moments later.

She felt numbed; it would take a while for the shock of this to wear off.

But looking down at the Deacon, she felt a strange and contradictory peace. He would live. She would see to that. And he would need her now, as she needed him.

A prayer formed on her lips as she looked toward the window. She did not hate that lonely, grim-faced man riding away. No, she felt sorry for him. . . .

IX

THE RAIN slanted against Ben's back as he rode, dripped from his hat brim, seeped down between poncho and coat collar to run icy fingers down his back. The brush flanking the road seemed to weep as he passed. Ahead, West Bend was lost to view at the base of the rain-swept hills.

Ben was aware of the weather now, where he had not been before—the ride back to town seemed longer, more dismal. The barely healed wound in his leg bothered him. He tried not to think beyond the return to his hotel room, a change into dry clothes, a warm meal.

He had a little money of his own, and Brazos' wallet containing the outlaw's share of the bank robbery. Ben had intended to turn this back to the bank, but now it no longer seemed to matter. He had not bothered to retrieve the money from the Deacon. Somehow, with the woman weeping over him, it would have seemed indecent.

It was the bank's money that had brought him to this; the bank could easily suffer the loss. Nor was vengeance still burning brightly within him. But he felt driven nonetheless to keep going, to find Johnson and the Kid. He couldn't stop to think, because to think was to open up the black pit of depression. He had to close his mind to keep going, although nothing much now seemed to matter.

The town appeared deserted when he rode in. He changed inside his room, stopped for a drink in the local bar. The liquor warmed him physically but did not lighten the deadness in his soul.

He ate a desultory meal in a restaurant run by an Irishman who seemed to take the weather as a personal affront and any reference to it by a stranger as an insult to Texas. He was, thought Ben, spoiling for a fight.

Maybe it's just the day, the ups and downs of everyday living, Ben reflected, and refused to be drawn into a quarrel which disappointed the brawny restaurant owner.

Ben paid his bill and walked to the stables, where he found his horse and Brazos' animal had been rubbed down and fed.

The stable hand was an old Navajo, brown-faced and wrinkled like a prune. Two black and intensely bright eyes looked deep into Ben's soul.

"Wait," he said. "No go now." He put a hand on Ben's arm, staying him. "In morning sun come—clouds go away—you feel better."

Ben paused. It was late in the day, and because of the rain it would be dark sooner than usual. What good would it do to ride into the night and finally to camp on wet ground?

Still, something deep and dark within him urged

him to push on. It wanted him to be miserable, to endure the worst. It wanted to destroy him, and Ben recognized it without intellectualizing.

He smiled at the Navajo stable hand, took his advice, and returned to his hotel room.

He slept fitfully, dreaming that he was chasing two men who only vaguely resembled Johnson and the Kid. They fled before him over dark and formless hills, and try as he might, he couldn't quite catch up. . . .

Ben woke in a sweat and knew that further sleep was impossible. It was still dark outside, but there was a wind pushing and slamming things and rattling his window panes. He dressed and went down to the lobby and left money with his key on the desk.

He glanced up as he stepped outside. The clouds were all but gone, scurrying before the wind. The rain had stopped. In the east, dawn was already flushing pink behind the lightness of emerging day.

He remembered the Navajo's words and shook his head.

He saddled by the light of a lantern left hanging on a hook in the stable. He knew the old Indian was watching, although he did not show himself. Ben left an extra silver dollar on the bench desk nailed to the wall and rode out.

The town was still sleeping as he headed south again, into Mexico.

• • •

THE ARROW arched down out of the blazing sun, slanting toward the two men huddled and trapped behind rocks. It slithered off one of the boulders, to bury its steel head into the hot sand a few feet beyond Johnson and the Kid.

The Kid kept his gaze fixed on the gully that made a crooked crack in the baked earth a hundred yards below him. Nothing moved. But he knew they were there—a half-dozen Apache warriors, waiting.

The dryness in his mouth reached down into his throat. The sun seemed to burn a hole through the back of his shirt. He said: "We can't just sit here, Hank. Let's make a break for it. There's only a half-dozen of them—"

"Not now," Hank interrupted. "Sun'll be going down in another three, four hours. We'll have a better chance then."

The Kid reached for his canteen, but Hank stopped him.

"But I'm thirsty," the Kid said angrily.

"So are they," Hank retorted. "Reckon we can wait as long as they can."

The Kid turned and glanced at something in the rocks behind them.

"Wonder how long *he* waited?"

Hank shrugged, not visibly concerned.

The dead man was no one they knew. He lay crumpled among the rocks a few yards behind them, the broken shaft of an Apache arrow still protruding from his side. His hair was sprinkled with gray; his clothes, which had seen much use, were nondescript.

The Kid eyed the corpse with an unfeeling gaze. It had been this man's firing that had drawn them into the trap, he reflected bitterly.

He and Hank had been riding toward the distant hills, heading for the village of Las Casitas somewhere ahead. They had learned this was where Major Sutter had gone into exile, a barren area in Mexico some fifty miles south of the Rio Grande. It was a place avoided by the Mexican *Federales,* for the two or three small villages within the area were too poor to merit government attention.

The Apaches found it a convenient sanctuary when hard pressed by the U.S. Cavalry.

Hank had picked up this information in Socorro, some twenty miles east of El Paso, where they had rested their horses and spent most of their money. They had been tempted to stay longer, but there was talk of trouble, of a "salt war" centered in El Paso, and the local peace officer, a hard-eyed man named Carl Webster, was cracking down on drifters.

No one had seemed quite sure what Major Sutter was doing in Mexico. Some rumors had it that he had a thousand men with him, ex-Confederate soldiers, disillusioned by Lee's surrender, turning away from their country. Some of the stories even held that Major Sutter was preparing to take over a large part of Chihuahua from Mexico, rule it as an independent country.

The thought had excited the Kid. However, Hank Johnson was a more practical man.

"We'll see what's going on when we get there, Kid," he had said.

He had been more worried about news that Tall Bear, one of Mangus Colorado's minor chiefs and a hot-headed Apache warrior, had eluded the Army and fled into Chihuahua with a band of young men.

But the ride in from Socorro had been uneventful . . . until this had happened.

They were lucky, Hank thought, to be alive. They had ridden unknowingly into the trap—the Kid's horse had been shot from under him before they realized what they had gotten into. He had taken the Kid aboard his own mount and they had made the shelter of the rocks just in time.

The man who had been trapped there by the Apaches was already dead when they got to him. But his horse was tied up in the rocks just behind. It was evident he had tried to pull the arrow from his side; it had broken off in his hands leaving the barb and a small part of the shaft still inside. He had slowly bled to death. . . .

Who he was, and why he was here, neither Johnson nor the Kid knew.

Johnson turned to look at the lowering sun. He had counted six warriors . . . he wasn't sure that was all of them.

"We'll make a run for it when it gets dark," he said. "If we have to split up, you know where to go." He pointed. "Major Sutter is somewhere in those hills."

The Kid nodded.

He could see his horse lying on its side . . . the sun glinted from the brass trumpet hanging from his saddle.

There was little he owned that had any value. But he would not ride out of here without that trumpet. . . .

He said: "Brazos is probably in Tampico right now. Having a hell of a time." His tone was hard, bitter.

"Maybe you should have stuck with him," Johnson said.

The Kid shook his head. "Too quick on the trigger for me. If he got to Tampico, he's in trouble. He always is, wherever he goes. . . ."

"*If* he made Tampico?" Johnson eyed the Kid.

The Kid's smile was crooked. "I was thinking of the sarge—"

An Apache showed up at the far end of the gully. He was looking toward a rocky ridge about a mile away where a smoke signal had blossomed against the sky. The puffs were like smoke from the mouth of a cannon. They were telling the warrior something, but neither the Kid nor Johnson could read them.

The warrior ducked back out of sight. Nothing moved for a long moment; then a rifle bullet cracked the stillness, the bullet slamming into the rock just above Hank's head. A moment later an arrow arced upward and came slithering down, landing uncomfortably close.

Both men gripped their rifles.

It was quiet again. Then hoofbeats sounded against the stillness. . . . The warriors appeared a few moments later, at the far end of the gully. They were moving away from them, heading for the distant ridge.

The Kid looked at Johnson.

"A trick?"

"Maybe."

They waited until the warriors faded from sight. Then they ran back to the horses, the Kid mounting the dead man's.

They rode out of the rocks, the Kid stopping by his dead horse to pick up his carbine, his saddle bags and his trumpet. They rode away from the ridge, keeping an eye on the smoke puffs.

Something had called the warriors away. Both men had an ominous premonition that whatever it was boded no good for them.

If they were going to join Major Sutter, they were going to have to go the long way around. . . .

X

SOCORRO BASKED in the hot sun, a few miles inside the Texas line and just far enough away from El Paso to be able to mind its own business. The town had been Mexican, as were all the border settlements, before Texas became first an independent republic and then, later, a state. It was still largely Mexican and thus influenced as much by events south of the border as by what went on north of it.

Reconstruction barely touched Socorro. There were a few mines just north of town, but cattle were beginning to become important. Ranchers were starting to pick up the pieces on ranges abandoned during the war. Maverickers were being shot or hung when caught by irate owners who could not or would not wait for the slower process of judicial law.

Drifters rode in and out of Socorro—broken men and angry men, displaced by war, uprooted and moving before the winds of chance.

Sheriff Carl Webster straddled his office doorway and looked down at the man who had just asked him a question he had heard many times since he had come to Socorro.

"Why?" he countered coolly. "Why do you want to know about Major Sutter?"

His badge glittered on his vest, its authority

supported by the revolver strapped in a holster to his thigh. He was a rangy man with a walrus mustache and flinty eyes, and he was about Ben's age.

"I served with him," Ben said. "I just wanted to know."

"There's been more than a dozen people asking the same thing," the sheriff said. "Two of them just last night."

Carl Webster came down the two steps from his office to stand facing Ben. "I never knew Major Sutter. Heard a lot of stories about him, though." His eyes held a cold distaste. "I don't like a man who quits his country because he lost a fight."

He waited for Ben to make something out of it, but as Ben remained silent, he continued: "All I know is that he and some others like him are holed up in some Mexican village south of here. A wagon used to come into Socorro once a month, for supplies. It's a week overdue now."

He shrugged. "Could be they're having trouble with the Mexican government."

"Or Apaches," Ben said. "Heard Tall Bear jumped the reservation at Fort Starke with about a hundred braves and headed south."

"Could be," Webster said. He took a cigar from his vest pocket and lighted it. "Not my worry, mister."

Ben turned his gaze south. Low, desolate hills thrust up against the horizon. Beyond was

Chihuahua, a hot, empty land and, as far as he was concerned, unknown territory.

"What's the name of the village? Las Casitas?"

"Was," the sheriff replied. "Heard the major renamed it Mecca." His grin was sour. "I hope the Mexican *Federales* run him and his ragtag bunch of exiles out of there."

"Know the way, Sheriff?"

Webster shook his head. "Fifty, maybe sixty miles south's all I know." He jerked a thumb in the direction of a Mexican restaurant down the street. "You could do what the others did—ask the Mexican cook in there. Name's Ramirez."

Ben nodded.

"The other two," he said soberly, "the ones who asked about Major Sutter last night? What'd they look like?"

The sheriff studied Ben closely now. He had been a lawman long enough to sense what was behind Ben's seemingly indifferent question.

"One was a tall, lanky sort of feller, middling thirties, I'd say. His companion was about twenty-one. Looked younger, though. Hard, both of them. The boy had a bugle tied to his saddle. Rode a splay-footed piebald mare. The older man rode a roan." He saw the look that flashed into Ben's eyes and his smile turned cold.

"If you start now, you'll be less than twenty-four hours behind them."

Ben's smile was small. "Much obliged, Sheriff."

The sheriff turned to go back inside his office. He stopped and looked at Ben. "Oh, keep an eye out for an old man left here this morning. One-armed man, balding, white-haired, driving a spring wagon." The sheriff shook his head. "Tried to talk him out of it, but the darn fool wouldn't listen. He's headed that way, too. . . ."

"I'll do that," Ben said.

He turned back to his horse and stood a moment by his saddle, eying the hills south of town. *Two down, two to go!* The small inner voice was insistent, prodding.

It was the only purpose he had in life now.

PEPE RAMIREZ, wiry, wizened, his brown face wrinkled, ageless, stuck his head out from the kitchen.

"Si," he answered Ben. But he waited until Ben dug out a silver dollar before he detailed the way to Las Casitas, the town he remembered.

"There is a small *rancho* on a creek about forty miles straight south. You follow the hills first, straight south. Keep the *montana* that looks like a saddle on your left, always. There is a wagon road, but it is easy to lose. When you get to the *rancho,* follow the arroyo toward the *montanas.* There, under the hills, *señor,* you will find Las Casitas."

Easy enough, Ben thought. But with a day's head start, the Kid and Johnson could beat him to Major Sutter.

He ate a meal at the counter, filled his two canteens, and left Socorro at the siesta hour. It was not the best time for travel in Chihuahua. But Ben was pressed for time, and there was nothing in Socorro to keep him.

An hour later Socorro had vanished from sight.

Riding, Ben was a mote in a vast and empty land seared by the sun—a land of thorny desert shrubs, of manzanita and catclaw, of volcanic hills that seemed as desolate and remote as the mountains on the moon.

Things lived here, but Ben wondered how. They hid from the sun in rock crevices and sand burrows—chuckwallas and desert iguanas, desert rats and collared lizards and sidewinders—somehow finding sustenance and water in a land largely barren and for much of the year blisteringly hostile.

He saw no signs of habitation, not even a goat-herd's shack, in his long ride south. But somewhere ahead was a small village—a Confederate outpost in Mexico; a sanctuary for adventurers, thieves and diehards.

Ben found it hard to believe that Major Sutter had brought his wife there, that the wives of many of the men who had followed the major had gone with them.

The sun went down over the western rim of the earth. Ben rested his horses (he still had Brazos' animal with him) and then rode on. The darkness softened the harshness of the land; the heat abated. He did not feel tired. But out of consideration for the animals, he forced himself to make camp around midnight. He slept lightly, and was on his way again before dawn.

The land began to shelve into what appeared to be a huge bowl rimmed on the south and west by distant mountains. He had seen no sign of life since leaving Socorro. Not until he suddenly ran across the wheel tracks of a wagon crossing a wash did he remember Sheriff Webster's mention of the old man who had left a few hours before him.

The tracks were fresh. Ben stared ahead, half expecting to see the wagon top the slight rise beyond the wash. *The man must have driven all night,* Ben thought, *to be still ahead of him. . . .*

He veered in now toward the hills that began to loom larger on the horizon. Not too far ahead, if Ramirez' instructions were correct, should be a small ranch. . . .

HE CAME UPON it suddenly, almost unexpectedly. The land dropped in front of him, and immediately below, nestling in the curve of a stream bed that ran dry for ten months of the year, was the ranch, or what was left of it!

The small pole corral still stood, partially shaded by a grove of cottonwoods, an adobe shed. The main house, probably not much larger than the shed, was a charred ruin.

Ben could see that much from where he paused—that, and the wagon parked in the yard.

Nothing moved.

The stillness of death seemed to hang over the place. Ben unsheathed his rifle and rode slowly down to the wagon.

The bays harnessed to the wagon turned to look at him as he approached. Ben pulled up alongside and glanced inside. . . . There was a small, battered trunk in the wagon bed, a blanket roll.

His eyes search the ruins. "Hey!" he called.

His voice seemed to vanish into the silence. He started to dismount, then suddenly whirled as he heard something off to the right.

The old man walked out from behind the shed and watched Ben. He stood silent, bareheaded, his scraggly long white hair stirring in the small wind that ran fitfully over the ruins. His left coat sleeve was empty. He was holding a shovel in his right hand.

He studied Ben for a moment, his eyes bright blue, somehow cold and sad.

"Where you headed, fella?"

"Same place you are," Ben replied. He lowered his rifle. "Sheriff in Socorro told me to keep an eye out for you."

"Don't need a wet nurse," the old man snapped. He motioned toward the shed. "There's another shovel in there. Give me a hand."

Ben frowned. "What're you digging?"

“Graves,” the old man said. “Four of them.” He turned his gaze to the hills, now less than ten miles away. “Smoke signals,” he said abruptly. “Been seeing them all morning. We’ll have to work fast.”

XI

THE RANCHER lay on his back, staring sightlessly at the sun, one hand curled around the broken shaft of an arrow in his chest. He was Mexican. So was his wife, spread-eagled and bloodied, just beyond. The body of their son, a small boy, lay just beyond her protective reach, pitifully crumpled and broken.

Ben said: "Where's the fourth?"

The old man motioned with the shovel. "Over there, by the trees. Young blond feller. . . ."

Ben turned quickly toward the cottonwood grove. *The Kid?* But the man lying face down was not one of the two he was after. He turned the man over and looked at him for a long moment, trying to picture his company bugler as he had known him. Even allowing for the passage of a few years, this was not the Kid.

The old man called: "You know him?"

Ben shook his head. He lifted the body across his shoulder and walked back, laying him alongside the others.

The one-armed man was trying to dig in the sandy bottom of a wash behind the shed, using his hip for leverage.

Ben took the shovel away from him. "First heavy rain and they'll float away," he pointed out. His tone was dry and noncommittal.

The old man shrugged. "Maybe. But we can't leave them out here for the coyotes and the buzzards." He pulled out a handkerchief and mopped his sweaty face. "Be on my conscience the rest of my life."

He reached for the shovel, but Ben pushed him away. "I told that sheriff in Socorro I'd look after you." He smiled. "Now go sit down somewhere. I'll do the digging."

The old man scratched his head. "You better hurry then," he said. "I've got a feeling they'll be back."

"Who?"

"Apaches," the old man replied. "Heard some of them jumped the reservation at Fort Starke and headed this way."

He watched as Ben took off his shirt and started to dig. Ben worked quickly, glad of a chance to loosen his muscles. The earth was soft, sandy—the sun was hot. Sweat glistened on his back, ran down his chest.

He dug the graves side by side and eased the bodies into them, one by one. He covered them quickly and then piled as many stones as he could find on each grave.

The old man came to stand by Ben when he finished. He looked down at the graves for a long moment, his lips moving in silent prayer.

He turned to Ben. "Should be some kind of marker for them," he said. "But we don't even know who they are."

Ben thought of the men he had seen blown to bits in the war, others killed and left to rot in swamps and pine woods—men unsung and unremembered.

"Doesn't really matter, does it?"

The old man watched him as Ben slipped into his shirt. "What you headed for Mecca for?"

"Some people I knew," Ben replied. "Heard they were coming here."

"Friends?"

Ben was looking off toward the hills, where a puff of smoke caught his attention.

"We were in the war together," he answered finally. Then, turning: "Maybe you're right about those Apaches coming back. Let's get out of here."

THEY FOLLOWED the arroyo toward the hills, moving with it as it twisted, turned and dipped through that barren land. Ben rode behind the wagon, alert and watchful. He knew enough about Apaches to know they did not send up smoke signals for nothing.

The Jalisco Mountains loomed up ahead, dry, rocky and forbidding. Somewhere within them was water, timber and grass. But the face they presented to Ben as he eyed them was barren and hostile.

The smoke signals were coming from the high ridges, which probably meant this was where Tall

Bear and his warriors had fled—a savage sanctuary just far enough from the border to stop pursuit by the U.S. Army and in an area remote enough to discourage ouster by the Mexican Federal troops.

Up ahead, the old man had stopped. He pointed as Ben rode alongside.

"Mecca," he said. "Looks like we're out of trouble."

Ben saw the town now—a scatter of toy adobes at the base of the hills. Some greenery showed, a welcome sight in that land where trees and water were scarce and precious.

The old man reached down for his canteen under the seat. He held it up, smiling. "Been saving it until I was sure." He tilted the canteen up, draining what was left.

Ben's gaze moved in a semicircle from the town. He was reaching for his own canteen when something caught his attention.

Riders! Two of them, although they were still too far away to make out who they were.

The old man lowered his canteen. "See something?"

Ben reached inside his saddle bag, took out his field glasses and studied the oncoming riders.

A tremor went through the long muscles of his back; he suddenly had difficulty swallowing. He dismounted, put the glasses away and drew his rifle.

The old man stared at him, alarm cracking his voice. "Apaches?"

Ben said harshly: "Just sit there, old man. Don't move! Don't say anything!"

He dipped down into the arroyo, out of sight.

HANK JOHNSON slowed his laboring mount to a walk and glanced at the Kid riding alongside. His tired face cracked in a relieved grin.

"Looks like we've run into some luck for a change."

The Kid studied the wagon and the two saddle horses up ahead. There was an old man on the seat, watching them. Something about one of those horses bothered him.

"That roan," he said, eying Hank. "Recognize it?"

Hank shook his head. They were moving at a walk now, the arroyo looming up just ahead. *Just in time,* he was thinking. The horse under him wouldn't last another mile. He glanced at the Kid. His animal was in better shape, but scarcely in condition to carry a double burden. Not if they had to make a run for it. And he had the decidedly uneasy feeling they soon would have to.

"Looks like the horse Brazos was riding," the Kid said.

Hank shook his head. "You're seeing things. Brazos is in Tampico by now. You said so yourself. . . ."

He turned his attention to the old man in the wagon. "Hey!" he called. "You going into Mecca?"

The old man didn't answer. He was staring into the arroyo, and the Kid suddenly pulled to a stop, something warning him.

"Hank!" he called bleakly. "I don't like—"

Ben came out of the arroyo then, moving quickly, his rifle ready and cocked. . . .

The Kid stiffened. Hank, turning, cursed. He dug spurs into his wind-broken animal and reached for his holster gun.

The animal plunged directly at Ben as Johnson, rising in his stirrups, fired wildly at the man he had not expected to see there.

Ben lunged aside, fired hastily; his bullet knocked Johnson out of the saddle. The roan, swerving abruptly away from Ben's muzzle flare, rammed into the Kid's piebald just as the Kid reached for his gun. The piebald went down in a crashing fall, pinning the Kid under him and momentarily knocking the wind from the younger man.

Ben walked to where Johnson lay crumpled, his right hand still clenched around his gun. It had been a lucky shot, Ben conceded. But he felt no regret as he bent over the body, pulled Johnson's gun from his grasp and tossed it away.

The piebald had scrambled to his feet and was running wildly, following Johnson's animal as it dipped down out of sight in some erosion gully beyond.

The Kid was stirring as Ben went to him. Ben took his gun, and stepped back as the Kid started to scramble to his feet.

"Hold it right there, mister!"

Ben turned his head to look at the old man standing up in the wagon. He was holding a double-barreled derringer in his hand, the twin muzzles pointed at Ben.

"He's only a boy," the old man said. "And I've had enough of killing."

The Kid staggered to his feet, groped at his empty holster; then, his gaze clearing, he stared bitterly at Ben.

"The Deacon said you'd come after us, Sarge. I thought he was crazy. So did Brazos." His gaze wandered to Johnson's body behind Ben, and bitterness crept into his voice.

"We almost made it, Hank. A few more miles—"

Ben made a motion with the Kid's Colt. "Let's go, Ira!"

A small shiver went through the Kid at the name. It had been a long time since he had been called that. *Ira Banning!* It was the name in his Army file. *Was it really his name?*

He liked the Kid better. The identity was rooted in the Army; it was what Johnson, Brazos and the Deacon had called him. Even Ben Rollins. . . .

He walked ahead of Ben toward the wagon and the horses Ben had tied to the tailgate. He paused by Brazos' roan and glanced back to Ben.

"Brazos never made it to Tampico," he said. It was not a question.

Ben shook his head. "He died in a small town called San Marcos."

"The Deacon?"

Ben shrugged. "I don't know," he said. "He was still alive when I left him."

He motioned to the wagon. "Put your hands on the wheel, Kid."

The old man looked down as Ben took a pair of handcuffs from his saddle bag. He had always carried them with him as a law officer, and he had forgotten to turn them in when he had left Spanish Wells.

"You a lawman?" the old man asked.

"I was."

The old man sighed as he slipped the derringer back into his coat pocket and settled on the wagon seat. "Glad you didn't kill him," he said. "I don't care what he did. . . ."

He watched Ben cuff the Kid's hands in front of him. A short length of chain linked them together, confining his movements but allowing the Kid to ride.

"Looks like we part company here," Ben said to the old man. "You oughta make it into Mecca without much trouble."

He motioned the Kid to Brazos' horse. "We're going back to Spanish Wells."

The Kid was staring past him, toward a distant ridge. He shook his head. "No," he said harshly. "We're not going back there! Not if you want to stay alive!"

He motioned with his cuffed hands. "That's what Hank and me was running from!"

Ben turned as the old man stiffened in his seat.

The scouting party that had pinned the Kid and Johnson down earlier had joined another small group. They topped the ridge now, began to slant down toward them.

The Kid turned and climbed up into the wagon. "You go ahead, Sarge," he sneered. "Maybe you can outrun them. But I'm going into Mecca!"

Ben cocked his pistol. "Get down!" he said grimly.

The Kid shook his head, a stubborn grin on his face. The old man took the derringer out of his pocket. "Let him stay!" His eyes were bright and hard. "Or you'll have to kill me, too!"

The Kid's glance went to the war party. He said quickly: "We ain't got much time, Sarge!"

Ben's jaw ridged. He did not want to go into Mecca, but he had no choice.

He eased the hammer back, slid his gun into the holster, and mounted.

The Kid said: "It's gonna be close, Sarge. Let me have Brazos' rifle?"

Ben eyed him.

"I'll give it back," the Kid promised, "soon as we get to Mecca!"

The old man picked up his reins. "We're going to need all the help we can get. Give it to him. You've got his word."

Ben handed the Kid the rifle. He knew what the Kid was thinking. In Major Sutter's town, he wouldn't need a rifle.

"I'll be riding behind you!" he said grimly. "Don't you forget it!"

XII

IT WAS A long five miles to the old Mexican village at the foot of the sun-baked Jaliscos.

The old man's bays put all they had into their wild run along the ancient river bed that curled and dipped across the desolate plain. It was a grueling ride, with the old man guiding the team with one hand, concentrating on keeping them from running into the arroyo as it twisted and turned in front of them.

The Kid rode the bouncing seat, the rifle in his hands. He watched the Apache war party as it slanted down from the ridge, heading to cut them off from Mecca.

Ben rode behind and to the far side of the Kid. He had his Colt in his right hand, but he knew the effects of whatever shooting he would do from the deck of a running horse would be more cautionary to the pursuing Apaches than accurate.

There were about a dozen warriors in the patrol. Two of them, mounted on faster horses, were beginning to pull away from their companions. They were cutting in toward the wagon from the right, their riders moving like part of the animals under them.

Ben swung his glance to Mecca. The town lay quiet in the desert sunlight, seemingly unaware of the life and death chase going on in front of it.

Why don't they see us? Ben thought.

But no one rode out to help.

The wagon bounced over an imbedded rock, flinging the old man on the seat. The reins slipped from his grasp. The Kid turned and caught them before they went over the side. He grinned as the old man regained his balance.

"Hang on!" he said. "We got it made, Pop!"

The old man took the reins from him as an arrow slammed into the side of the wagon. The Kid swiveled, aimed and fired. The Apache brave, less than fifty feet away, slid limply from the back of his running horse.

The other warrior loosed an arrow at the Kid just as Ben fired three shots at him. The third one knocked the brave off his horse, sending his arrow arcing high over the wagon.

Ben glanced back. The remaining warriors were coming up fast. . . .

They were approaching the town now, and still it was strangely quiet. The main street cutting through Mecca appeared deserted.

Had Major Sutter and his men abandoned it?

Then, as though answering them, a bugle sounded, thin, uncertain, yet trembling defiantly above the roof tops.

The rifles opened up above them as the wagon and Ben swept past the first buildings into town. It was a ragged but determined volley, and Ben, glancing upward, glimpsed Confederate uniforms on the flat roofs, firing at the pursuing Apaches from behind the protection of low adobe parapets.

The angry patrol broke and turned back. Rifle fire reached after them. But the marksmanship was poor. The braves made it beyond rifle range, where they regrouped for a moment, eying the village. Then the leader shook his fist in a gesture of defiance, and they rode off toward the flanking, desolate hills.

AHEAD OF BEN, the wagon was slowing; it pulled to a stop by a building midway down the deserted street. Ben rode slowly now, his gaze roaming the quiet buildings. It was not much of a town; hardly the place that could house an army of exiles. It did not even look lived in. Many of the windows of the lower floors were boarded up, their occupants evidently having moved out. . . .

Ben rode alongside the wagon and glanced at the Kid and the old man. Behind them the firing had stopped. The silence seemed to press around them, dispelling the notion that there had been any firing at all.

The Kid was eying the quiet buildings, an uneasy expression in his eyes. The old man sagged back on the seat, spent, his lined face grim.

"Where's everybody?" the Kid asked. He turned to look at Ben. "You must've heard them, Sarge. The bugle? The rifle fire?"

Ben nodded.

The old man looked frightened. "Maybe we've come to the wrong place. Maybe this isn't Mecca—"

"I don't know about Mecca," Ben cut in grimly. "But this is where Major Sutter came after the war." He pointed to something down the street. "Nobody else would have hung out that sign."

The Kid followed the old man's gaze to the canvas sign strung across the street. It hung limply in the late morning heat.

WELCOME TO THE HOME
OF
THE FIFTH TEXAS CAVALRY

But there was no welcome for them. The sign hung like yesterday's vain hopes across the deserted street. A ghostly silence pervaded the village where Major Sutter had come to live, to plan an empire in the Mexican desert.

The Kid gripped his rifle, his eyes hard, fighting the flicker of uncertainty. "Hey!" he called. He stood up in the wagon and raised his voice. "Hey! Where's everybody?"

The silence swallowed his voice.

The Kid brushed a hand across his eyes. "Sarge—" he said, looking at the grim-faced rider next to him. His voice came through dry lips. "We dreaming, Sarge?"

A door creaked in the stillness. The Kid

swiveled around, bringing his rifle muzzle up. Ben's hand dropped to his gun butt.

The sound came from across the street, from a building that once had served as a Mexican cantina. But the sign above the batwing doors read:

WELCOME FIFTH CAV
Tom Starbright, Prop.

A solid oak door, usually closed only at night or during emergencies, was opening inward, creaking on seldom used hinges. A man was coming through—a tall, cadaverous-looking man with a bottle of whiskey in his hand.

Ben started. If, at the moment, Mecca gave him the feeling of a dead town, the man behind the opening door could well have risen from the grave!

He paused, his long thin arms draped loosely over the tops of the batwings. Emaciated, ageless, clad in cast-off clothing, the man surveyed them with sardonic amusement. Then, slowly, he shuffled out to the walk in front of the saloon, blinking as the fierce sunlight hit his face. He pawed at it with the bottle as though to push the brightness away.

Then, holding his forearm up to shade his eyes, he greeted them. "Welcome to Mecca, pilgrims." But his voice was hollow, mocking.

The Kid lowered his rifle and glanced uneasily at Ben. Ben turned his mount and started to ride toward the man.

The man waved him back. "That's close enough, mister." His voice was thin, cracked. "Wouldn't want you to get into trouble. . . ."

Ben pulled up in the middle of the street. "Where're the others?"

"Others?" The man looked at Ben with blurred sadness. "Ain't nobody else, mister. Just me—Smith. Just me. . . ."

Ben was puzzled. "Where's Major Sutter? The soldiers we saw on the roofs—"

The man who called himself Smith shook his head. "No soldiers here." He lifted the whiskey bottle to his lips and slobbered some of it down his chin. "You should have stayed away, mister; ain't nothing here now."

Ben stared angrily at the man. *Was he just drunk?*

Behind him, the Kid said: "Why, someone blew a bugle call as we drove into town. And I saw soldiers up on those roofs—"

A voice cut in from somewhere up the street. It was sharp, commanding.

"You there! Get that wagon off the street!"

Ben swung around. A hundred yards up the street, a figure in a Confederate uniform stood in the shadow of a doorway. The figure was motioning with the muzzle of a rifle.

"Drive down that alley!" it instructed. "There's a stable in back!" Urgency sharpened the high-pitched voice. "Hurry!"

The Kid started to climb down from the wagon, a grin on his face. "Major Sutter?"

The voice stopped him, the rifle muzzle threatening. "Down the alley! We'll talk later!"

The Kid settled back on the seat. The old man slapped the ends of his reins across the rump of the horses. The team lurched forward. He turned them into the alley indicated by the uniformed figure.

Ben rode behind the wagon, cutting away from it as it turned toward the stables and moving toward the uniformed figure. The face under the officer's cap was not readily distinguishable.

"You, too!" the figure ordered. The rifle muzzle steadied on him. "Get those horses out of sight!"

Ben eyed the mysterious figure for a moment, trying to make out the features of Major Sutter. He had not known the major very well. . . . Sutter had been a cold, bloodless sort who stood apart from his command.

"Hurry!" the figure said, and there was a note of desperation in the voice.

Ben shrugged; he turned and followed the wagon down the alley.

The figure in the shadows waited until he had gone out of sight. Then it stepped out into the street, the harsher sunlight outlining a slender, almost boyish figure.

Smith stared at the figure, a nameless dread in his eyes.

"Get back inside!" the voice ordered.

Smith waved the bottle at the officer. "Dead!" he called. "You're all dead!" His voice was thin, reedy; like the bugle call, it trembled on the heavy stillness. "All dead."

He turned then as the figure took a step toward him and stumbled back into the saloon, the heavy door creaking, slamming shut behind him.

XIII

THE STABLE smelled of recent occupancy, although it was empty now. The heat of midday seemed concentrated within it. The old man looped his reins around the whipstock and loosened his black string tie and collar. He was tired and bewildered and crushed by the silence and the strangeness of the town.

The Kid sat on the wagon seat and waited for Ben to ride up. He had the rifle across his lap, and his eyes were hard and unforgiving.

Ben dismounted. He was uneasy about the place, uneasy about the Kid.

He said: "All right, Kid." He held out his hand. "Give me the rifle."

The Kid eyed him with a bright cold stare. "No," he said. His voice was flat and final.

Ben took a deep breath. "You ran with the wrong company too long, I reckon. There was a time when you would have stayed with your word."

"It was a long time ago, and a different kind of world," the Kid replied. The chain links on his manacles clinked softly as he shifted the rifle muzzle to target Ben.

"You shot Hank," he continued, his voice harsh, bitter.

"And Brazos and the Deacon." Ben's voice was even, without regret. "Johnson was no better—"

"He was the only kin I had. I didn't care about Brazos or the Deacon. But me and Hank—" the Kid's voice was softly bitter— "we were going to take the world by the tail—"

"By robbing a bank? Killing people?" Ben's voice was harsh.

"We were broke," the Kid said. "It seemed like the thing to do—"

Ben took a step forward. "Johnson's dead," he said coldly. "I could have left you out there, for the Apaches—"

The Kid's thumb drew back the hammer. "Maybe you should have, Sarge. . . ." His eyes were bright and unrelenting. "Maybe you should have!"

The old man stirred and put his hand inside his coat pocket. He said: "This is no time for argument, Kid. Give him back his rifle."

The Kid shot him a look. His eyes narrowed as he saw the derringer in the old man's hand.

"You taking his side, old man?"

"I'm taking nobody's side," the man said. "But you gave him your word back there—"

The Kid's fingers tightened on the rifle. "Who cares about you, old man!" he shot back. "Shoot if you want! But I'm keeping this rifle—"

There was movement now in the alley behind them. The Kid's glance shot past Ben to the figure coming toward them.

"Major Sutter?"

Ben turned.

The uniformed figure stopped in a patch of sunlight a dozen feet from the stable door. A hand reached up in a tired gesture and pulled the cap away from her head. A mass of yellow hair tumbled to the woman's shoulders.

"Sorry I acted sharply back there," she said. "But it was necessary to get you off the street." She managed a small smile at the look in their eyes.

"I'm Laurie Sutter—Major Sutter's widow."

The Kid's eyes narrowed. "The major's dead?"

She nodded slowly; for a moment an old hurt showed in her eyes. Then she became businesslike as she walked toward them.

"You came alone? Just the three of you?"

Ben said quietly: "Yes. Just the three of us."

She slid her rifle down by her feet and leaned against the door framing, sharp disappointment in her eyes.

"I was hoping that someone from Socorro would miss us—"

"I was in Socorro," the old man said. "Nobody there cared—" He took a deep breath. "I'm Thorne Selby, ma'am. You may have heard of me."

Laurie Sutter shook her head.

"My sister's here. She's expecting me."

"I'm sorry," Laurie said. She turned to Ben.

"Why did you come?"

Ben shrugged. “I didn’t want to come here, ma’am.” He glanced at the Kid. “But he was headed this way.”

“Oh!” Laurie Sutter seemed to notice the manacles on the Kid’s wrists for the first time. “He your prisoner?”

Ben nodded. He looked past her, up the alley toward the street. Somewhere in town a baby started to cry. It seemed strangely out of place in the odd, depressing stillness.

“Your uniform, Mrs. Sutter?” He eyed her, frowning. “Why the masquerade?”

Laurie looked off across the roof tops. A bitter smile touched her lips. “You’re right: it is a masquerade, all of it, complete with bugle calls and rifle fire. But it’s kept us alive. . . .”

Her shoulders sagged as the strain of the past days got through to her. She was silent for a long moment, her hands tightened about the barrel of her rifle.

The Kid stood up, the rifle held firmly in his hands. “I don’t know what’s going on here,” he said harshly. “But it ain’t what I was coming here for—”

He stiffened as he felt the twin muzzles of the derringer press against the small of his back.

“It isn’t what I expected, either,” Selby said. “Drop the rifle!”

The Kid turned to look at him, and Ben moved quickly, reaching up and twisting the rifle from his hands. He stepped back, glancing at the woman in the doorway.

"It wasn't my idea, coming here," he said. "I never liked your husband, and the war ended for me at Appomattox." He turned to the Kid, motioned him down from the wagon.

"Let's get out of here!"

The woman said: "I'm sorry. But I'm afraid you'll have to stay, whoever you are—"

"Ben Rollins." He eyed the rifle she held. "Why?" His voice was hard. "You're not going to try to keep me here, are you, Mrs. Sutter?"

She shook her head. "Not I. But you're trapped here—like the rest of us. Those savages that chased you into Mecca have us penned in. They're in the hills behind us, waiting. Their patrols are out on the plain, watching." She paused, brushed hair from her face. "We've been waiting three days for help out of Socorro—or for troops from Fort Starke."

Ben's eyes narrowed. "This is Mexico, ma'am. Why would troopers from Fort Starke come down here?"

"Because Tall Bear is here. Out there in the hills. And we're United States citizens—"

"What about the soldiers right here?" the Kid interrupted savagely. "The ones we saw on the roofs? What the devil are they doing?"

Laurie looked at him. "Soldiers? There are no soldiers here!"

"That sign out there!" The Kid's voice was bitter. "Home of the Fifth Cav! Major Sutter's old outfit!"

Laurie Sutter shook her head. "There are no soldiers in Mecca." She turned and motioned down the alley.

"Look!"

Women were straggling down the alley toward them. They were of various ages, from twenty to their mid-forties; one or two older. All of them were wearing parts of Confederate uniforms, tunics mostly, caps, whatever fitted. All of them carried rifles.

They came to stand behind Laurie, eying the men inside. They looked exhausted, red-eyed from lack of sleep, strained to the breaking point. Behind them appeared two old men, gray-bearded, with straggly white hair. They came to stand with the women. With them was a boy, not more than ten—a slender, tow-haired child clutching a battered Army bugle.

"Here are your soldiers," Laurie said. "A handful of women, two old men and—" she paused, her voice sinking— "a boy with a bugle."

Selby stared. "But your men, Mrs. Sutter? My sister's husband? Where are *they?*"

"Dead, most of them. The others are in there. . . ." Laurie pointed to the back of the building from which she and the others had emerged. "They're in there—dying."

Selby's voice was shocked. "Wounded?"

Laurie shook her head.

"For God's sakes, Mrs. Sutter!" Selby exploded. "What is it then?"

Laurie eyed him for a moment; then: "I think it's typhoid."

Ben took an involuntary step away from her; the Kid pressed back against the wagon. Typhoid was a mean word on the frontier.

The Kid said slowly: "You mean there's just you, ma'am? And them? Against Tall Bear?"

Laurie did not bother to reply.

Selby climbed down from the wagon. "There's not much that can be done for typhoid," he said. "But I'll see what I can do."

Laurie frowned. "Thank you," she said. "But I'm afraid there's little you—"

"I said I'd see them!" the old man said stiffly. "I was an Army surgeon not too long ago. I haven't forgotten all I learned."

He walked past her into the alley.

Laurie looked at Ben. "You still want to leave?"

Ben eyed the frightened women behind her. "Not much choice, have we, Mrs. Sutter?"

He turned to the Kid. "Looks like we're staying. . . ."

XIV

THE SIGN over the balcony facing the street read: HOTEL MECCA. It was one of several two-story buildings in town, enlarged and repaired by the men who had followed Major Sutter to the abandoned Mexican village.

There was a long room behind the small lobby; it had been, until recently, the hotel dining room. And Major Sutter had held his meetings there.

Now it was filled with sick men. Most of the chairs and tables had been removed, and cots lined the walls, so that it resembled a hospital ward.

Selby paused by the closed door with Laurie and looked at the stout woman standing guard.

"Let him in, Emma," Laurie said. "He's a doctor."

Emma opened the door and stepped aside. "Mrs. Devereaux is in there with them," Laurie told the doctor. "She's had some nursing experience." She paused. "Her husband was among the first to die."

Selby nodded. "Keep everyone away. I'll see what I can do."

Emma closed the door behind him and stood in front of it, a big, graying woman with sad eyes.

The women and the old men who had followed them into the lobby stood behind Laurie. They waited, helpless without direction.

Ben, standing to one side with the Kid, watched

as a young woman pushed her way through the others toward the door.

Laurie stepped in front of her. "Cindy!"

The younger woman tried to push her aside. "I've got to see my husband! I've got to go in there—"

"You know the rules!" Laurie cut in sharply. "No one goes inside except Mrs. Devereaux!"

Cindy struggled to get past Laurie. Emma moved in to help Mrs. Sutter.

"I must see if Bill is still alive!" She turned on Laurie, despair in her eyes. "You've no right to keep me from him!"

"There's nothing you can do for him," Laurie said.

"I can be *with* him!" Cindy cried. The strain of the past days was taking its toll; she was beginning to crack. "That's what's important to me, Mrs. Sutter—just to be with him!" Her voice broke. "Oh, my God! I don't care about the risk to me. Bill needs me!"

"The risk is to all of us!" Laurie said firmly. "I can't let you go in there." She tried to get through to the distrait woman with reason. "Your husband needs you, Cindy. But not in there, weeping by his side."

Cindy pulled back from Laurie, her lips trembling. "Maybe tears are all I can give Bill now. But it's more than you gave your husband, isn't it, Mrs. Sutter?"

"Cindy!" Emma's voice was rough, disapproving.

Cindy ignored the older woman. "Major Sutter died in that room, Emma. Without her." She turned to the woman in the lobby behind her. "The major died with only Mrs. Devereaux by his side. He knew he was dying. But he didn't ask for his wife." She turned back to face Laurie. "He didn't ask for you, because he didn't want you—"

Her voice broke now, her tears and her fears overwhelming her.

"My God! He didn't even want you while he lay there dying!"

Laurie stood stiffly by the door, watching the weeping woman. For a brief moment the mask of hard self-sufficiency cracked, and her eyes reflected an inner, secret torment.

Then, harshly, she took control of herself, of the situation.

"Emma!" she called. Her voice was icy, commanding. "Take Cindy upstairs!"

Cindy jerked her arm free as the woman took hold of her. She seemed suddenly to become aware of the rifle she still clutched, part of the grim masquerade in which she was participating.

In sudden rebellion she flung it away from her, toward the window facing the street.

"If Bill dies," she cried helplessly, "I won't care what happens to me—to any of you!"

Emma took her arm again, holding her gently.

"We know, Cindy," she said softly, "we know." She looked at Laurie. "I'll stay with her for a while."

Laurie nodded. She turned away toward the closed door to hide the bright shine of unshed tears that welled up in her eyes.

BEN WAS standing by the hotel desk with the Kid, watching Laurie. *A remarkable woman,* he thought. *A ragtag bunch of women, about to come apart under fear and strain—how long had she held them together?*

The Kid moved restlessly beside him. "How about taking these off, Sarge?" He held up his manacled hands.

Ben shook his head.

"A hundred Apaches out there," the Kid snarled, "waiting to take over this town! Give me a gun, Sarge!"

Ben shook his head. "I did, once. I can't trust you now!"

"Then get me out of here!" the Kid said bitterly. "Put me on a horse, and let's make a break for it!"

He moved closer as Ben did not answer. "That's what you came after, wasn't it? Me, Hank, Brazos and the Deacon! Well, I'm the only one left. What are you gonna do with me?"

"I don't know," Ben said slowly. He glanced toward the window, seeing in his mind's eye the dry, rocky hills beyond. "Right now it doesn't seem to matter."

He turned as Laurie started moving among the silent women. "Everyone back to her post," she was saying. "Those on rest call go to their rooms. I'll see that you're awakened for your turn on the roof."

The women began to move away, some toward the back door, a few others dragging themselves wearily up the lobby stairs.

Zeb Lowden shuffled toward Ben and the Kid. He was a long-shanked, dried-up sort of man with a stoop to his shoulders. The rifle he dragged, butt down, behind him seemed too heavy for him. He had pouches under his eyes, dark from lack of sleep. Those pale eyes searched Ben's face with a deep anxiety.

"You come from Socorro?"

Ben nodded.

"See anyone on the way?" His eyes seemed to wander as he talked; there was a tired ring to his voice.

"Nobody alive," Ben said.

"A yellow-haired boy, 'bout twenty? Name's Joe. He rode out of here day before yesterday. Gonna get help in Socorro." He plucked at Ben's arm pleadingly. "You musta seen him."

Ben looked away, not wanting to answer.

"My grandson," Zeb persisted. "Just a boy. Blond hair, blue eyes. Laughed a lot. . . ."

"He's dead," Ben said quietly.

The old man pulled back as though he had been struck a blow.

"Joe? You sure? He was mounted on a fast horse—"

"A gray mare, branded Double X on the right shoulder." Ben's voice held no emotion. "He didn't get beyond the Mexican *rancho* on the creek out there."

Zeb's hand trembled as he brushed it across his eyes. "Not Joe—" He turned away, stumbling toward the back door. "Not Joe—"

Laurie paused by the desk, looking after him. "You didn't have to tell him," she accused. "You could have left him some hope."

"What good would it do?"

The spark of anger faded in Laurie. She was very tired; so she did not want to argue with this big man.

"There was another man who rode out for help. Caleb Brooks. He was about forty-five, with graying hair, a small mole on the side of his neck—"

The Kid began to laugh; a joyless, bitter sound. "He's dead, too, ma'am. Up behind that long ridge out there."

"Joe and Caleb—they were the only two able-bodied men left. They volunteered. . . ."

She looked at Ben and the Kid, hating them for their seeming indifference.

The dining room door opened, and Doctor Selby came into the lobby. He seemed to have revived. His step was steady, his tone brisk.

He looked at Ben. "My bag's in the wagon, locked up in my trunk. Give me a hand with it?"

Ben nodded.

Laurie said: "How bad is it in there?"

Selby cracked a smile. "With God's help, most of them will live."

Ben waited for him at the back door; they went out together.

Laurie started for the stairs. She stopped as the Kid stepped in front of her.

She gave him a cold look. "I'm tired," she said. "If you don't mind, I'm going up to my room."

The Kid held up his hands. "I want to get out of these."

She sighed. "You'll have to talk to the man who put them there. Nothing I can do." She started past him, paused, and looked back, a flicker of curiosity in her eyes. "What did you do?"

"Robbed a bank," the Kid said. "Blew my share in Socorro." He eyed her indifferently. "Is there a blacksmith shop in town?"

She didn't answer him.

His tone hardened. "I'm not staying here, ma'am."

"Why did you come?"

"I was a bugler in the war. Major Sutter was my commanding officer." He shrugged. "I was on the run, and this seemed like a good place to come to."

He held up his hands again, yanking at the iron links. "Now be a good lady, ma'am. Help me get out of these!"

Laurie shook her head. "My husband's dead. I don't know what he would have done with you. But I can't help you."

She pushed past him and went upstairs.

The Kid looked after her, bitter anger in his gaze. "Welcome to the home of the Fifth Cav," he sneered. "A thousand soldiers waiting to take over Chihuahua. . . ." He walked to the window and looked outside.

The street was deserted. The banner across the street flapped in a gust of wind.

"Good thing you're dead, Hank!" He shook his clenched fists toward the hills he could not see. "You hear me! We came seven hundred miles for nothing—seven hundred miles to find none of what we'd heard was true!"

A wind was beginning to move along the street, blowing sand, rustling bits of paper; the banner flapped emptily above the deserted street.

The Kid turned away from the window and suddenly stopped, his gaze picking up the rifle Cindy Ellis had discarded. It lay against the back wall, most of it hidden under an old sofa. The Kid's gaze jumped to the back door.

Ben would be coming back with the one-armed

doctor. He strode quickly to the sofa, pulled the rifle out, checked it. There was a round in the chamber. That was all he needed.

His eyes gleamed recklessly as he turned and went out through the back door.

XV

CINDY ELLIS was lying face down on her bed, her face buried in her pillow. It was a small, cheerless room; despite her presence, and that of the older woman standing by the bed, it seemed depressingly empty.

There was a picture on the bedside table—a daguerreotype of a wedding. Herself and Bill, stiff in their formal pose.

All the bright hopes with which they had come there had vanished—the dreams and the plans and the promise of a new, exciting life. . . .

The door opened, and Laurie came into the room. Cindy either did not hear or did not care. Laurie made a motion to Emma, and the older woman nodded and left the room.

Laurie walked to the bed and put a hand on Cindy's shoulder.

"Cindy." Her voice was gentle.

Cindy turned and looked at her. She reacted hostilely as she saw who it was, rolled away from Laurie to the other side of the bed and got to her feet, facing the major's widow.

"What do you want?"

"Want?" Laurie was silent for a moment; then: "Nothing, really."

Cindy eyed her bitterly. "You came here to tell me that?"

"I came to see how you were."

"I'm fine," Cindy said. Her voice was defiant. "And I'll take my turn on the roof, like I always have."

Laurie sighed. "I know you will."

The defiance in the younger woman faded. "Bill's going to die, isn't he?"

"I don't know."

Laurie walked to the window and looked down into the street, which was silent, deserted, still. She raised her gaze to the hostile hills beyond.

They were there, waiting—the Apaches. The masquerade had kept them back up to now. But how long would Tall Bear wait?

Laurie turned to look back at the younger woman. "There are some things worse than death," she said.

Cindy's hands fisted helplessly. "It's all right for you to say that, Mrs. Sutter. You're old; you've had your life!"

Laurie's fingers went up to her cheek, to the small sun wrinkles around her eyes. She was thirty, but she *was* old to this girl.

Her smile had a touch of sadness.

"You've been married almost ten years," Cindy went on bitterly. "But I've been Bill's wife less than six months!"

She walked around the bed to join Laurie at the window, looked down on the town that was now a trap.

"Mecca!" She turned on Laurie in hopeless frustration. "We were on our way to California, Mrs. Sutter! Bill and I. But your husband met our wagon at Cedar Junction; he talked Bill into coming here. He painted a glowing picture of Mecca's future, of the unlimited possibilities."

Laurie let her speak.

"I tried to talk Bill out of it. But your husband touched on Bill's pride as a Texan, a Southerner. Mecca was the place to start again, free of Yankee rule, yet close enough to Texas to keep our ties—"

Cindy paused, emotion choking her.

Laurie nodded slowly. "Yes. Calvin could be a convincing speaker about Mecca."

She turned and looked out of the window again. There was strength in this woman, and it showed now through the strain and uncertainty of the moments ahead.

"But Calvin was right about the desert here, about Mecca. There is beauty here—and peace." She smiled at the irony of it now. "It was a chance for all of us to take a good long look at ourselves, to see what the war meant, what we now wanted to do. It gave those of us who came here a chance to start life anew. And maybe, some day, even opportunity—"

"For whom?" Cindy interrupted harshly. "For the dead?"

She walked away from Laurie, to stand by the

small dresser, staring into the mirror and seeing a twenty-year-old girl turned older by worry and bitterness and hopes destroyed.

"I'm no longer interested in the future, Mrs. Sutter. All that counts is now, today, tomorrow." She turned, her voice rising. "That's all there is to life—the *now!* The future is smoke, like those signals rising from—" she made a sharp gesture toward the window— "those hills!"

Laurie turned away from the look in her eyes, feeling sorry for this young woman, but knowing there was nothing she could do to ease the pain or change what had happened.

"We didn't even have much of a chance to get to know each other," Cindy went on. She closed her eyes against the start of tears; there was a heaviness in her chest, suffocating her. "I don't feel married, Mrs. Sutter. I don't feel anything!"

Laurie turned to go to her, but Cindy waved her away. "If you don't mind," she rebuffed her, "I want to be left alone!"

Laurie hesitated.

"Please!"

Laurie nodded and left the room.

BEN ROLLINS eased the small trunk out of the back of Selby's wagon and set it down at the doctor's feet. He had unhitched the team and stalled them, pitching in some hay and meting water to them from a barrel that stood by the stable door. And now he was doing the same to his horse and the one Brazos had ridden as far as San Marcos.

It was quiet in the alley; shadows were beginning to fill the narrow space as the sun slid down toward the western hills.

It was not what he had expected. He had come to Mecca prepared to face Major Sutter and a group of exiles, some of them former soldiers in arms. He had expected they would surely try to keep him from taking the Kid back to Spanish Wells. He had come to Mecca expecting almost anything but this.

A dying town defended by less than a score of women, two old men and a boy; a charade played under a hot desert sun in Mexico.

He had come a long way, Ben thought sourly, to die—but the possibility did not particularly jolt him. He had not really cared what happened to him since he had buried Sue.

He came back and stopped by Thorne Selby, who had opened the trunk and was kneeling beside it. Ben saw a family picture in a peeling gilt frame on top of folded clothing. Selby stared at it for a long moment, reflecting; then he pushed the picture aside and started to dig under the clothing, finding the scuffed black doctor's bag he had kept out of sentiment but had not expected to use again.

Ben said: "Anything in there that will help?"

"Typhoid?" Selby shrugged. "Very little. Some

day—maybe." He shook his head. "I haven't kept up with medicine for several years now."

He dropped the trunk lid, straightened. "I wasn't coming here as a doctor. I never wanted to use this again. My sister wrote; said she and her husband were joining Major Sutter down here. She begged me to come. I hadn't seen her in a long time, not since she married."

He sat down on the trunk, a tired old man who did not care much what happened to him.

"I don't even know if she's alive. I didn't see her among the women in there. Or her husband—" He ran his fingers through his straggly hair. "My wife died before the war. My two sons were killed at Cemetery Ridge." He glanced at his empty sleeve. "Got discharged after Sherman burned Richmond, where I lost this. I thought I'd come down here to sit in the sun and forget. . . ."

Ben shifted his position slightly. He could hear the baby crying again somewhere, and he thought emptily of life and death.

"Sorry," he said softly, "but it looks like none of us will have a chance to sit in the sun and rest."

"Not much we can do, is there?" the old man said.

Ben shrugged. "Looks like the women have about reached the end of their rope. They're depending on us now—you, me and—"

"Count *me* out!" the Kid said. His voice was hard and bitter.

He stood in the doorway behind them, the rifle cocked and deadly in his hands. "Save it!" he warned sharply as Ben made an instinctive move toward his holstered gun. "Save it for the Apaches, Sarge!"

Ben watched him, his eyes cold. The Kid moved toward them, his gaze on Selby.

"So they kicked you out of the Army, eh? Just military surplus, Doc—like me, Hank, the Deacon and Brazos." There was a hard, grating edge to his voice. "The war was over, and nobody wanted us any more. In the beginning, they gave us guns and said: 'Shoot the Yankees!' But when it was all over, they tried to take the guns away and give us nothin."

"Go ahead, Kid," Ben said contemptuously. "Get it out of your system."

The Kid turned a bitter glance on him. "Hell with you, Sarge!"

"You were just a boy when I knew you," Ben said, "a boy with a bugle. But even then you hung around the wrong crowd—the whiners and the malcontents—"

"Like Hank?" the Kid said in a brittle tone, and his eyes were hard and dangerous on Ben.

"Like Hank," Ben said coldly. "And Brazos."

"And the Deacon?" the Kid said softly. "What about him?"

"I don't know about the Deacon," Ben said. "He was a hard man to figure."

The Kid moved back a step and made a motion with the rifle. "I didn't come here to hear old Army stories," he snapped. "All I want is to get out of here! Now give the old man the key to these things so I can leave!"

Ben grinned. "Sorry. They're still in my old desk in Spanish Wells, Kid. Always kept them there."

The Kid's eyes flared dangerously. "You're lying!"

Ben shrugged. "Why should I?"

The Kid considered this for a moment. "All right," he said harshly, "I'll go with that." He motioned again with the rifle. "Put yore gun on that trunk, Sarge. Then step away, nice and easy."

Ben eased his gun from the holster, placed it on the trunk and moved away. He watched the Kid step forward, drop the rifle, quickly pick up Ben's gun, check the loads, cock it.

"Just a loan, Sarge," he said. "You'll get it back."

He turned his attention to Selby. "Almost forgot that popgun you carry, Doc. Toss it out there—in the hay!"

Selby did as directed.

The Kid grinned cockily. "Well, now," he said, "let's all take a walk."

Selby demurred. "I've got to get back inside—"

The Kid cut him off. "They can wait a few minutes." He motioned with the gun. "Not that I don't trust you, Doc. But you might just be tempted to make a fool of yoreself."

Ben said: "Where are we going?"

"There's a blacksmith shop up the street." The Kid held up his manacled hands. "To get rid of these!"

XVI

THE SUN beat down over the flat roofs of Mecca, searing the skin. Here and there on the roofs women in ill-fitting tunics, with hair pushed up under forage caps, watched through bloodshot, aching eyes, hands gripped around the unfamiliar stocks of rifles. They watched with terror in their hearts and hope fading from their thoughts.

There was water and food enough to hold out for weeks, but time, they knew, was running out. Tall Bear's foraying patrols were getting bolder. . . . Sooner or later a scout or two would get past them into the village and unmask the pitiful charade.

Zeb Lowden sat with his back supported by the parapet of what had been the village granary. From there he could keep an eye on both the hills and the eroded plain. He could see, if he wished, the beans drying on their stalks in rows just below the creek bed, the corn rustling in the wind.

There was water there, strangely enough, seeping up from some runoff of the Jaliscos—water channeled and brought into the fields through old irrigation ditches constructed by the Mexicans, who had finally abandoned them.

Zeb shifted his back against the crumbling adobe wall and stared with unseeing eyes toward the hills. There was a deep pain inside him as he waited, his rifle clasped between his legs. He was just shy of seventy, stringy and weather-toughened. His grandson had been all he had left of close kin. . . .

The boy came crawling toward him along the roofs. He carried a full canteen of water, and the bugle slung across his shoulder glinted in the sunlight.

He stopped by the old man and peered cautiously over the parapet.

"See anything, Jimmy?" Zeb's voice was tired, uncaring.

Jimmy was wiry, leggy, his hair bleached by long exposure to the sun. He scanned the hills, the long run of the desert plain. There was nothing to see except the hot, empty land. Yet the very absence of movement made those hills the more sinister, the plain more deadly.

He settled back beside the old man, placing the full canteen beside him.

"No more smoke signals?"

Jimmy shook his head. If he had been a few years younger, he might have taken this as a game. But he was just old enough to understand the danger, old enough to be frightened.

"Think they've gone away?" he asked.

Zeb remained with his head sunk on his chest. He didn't answer, and the boy became alarmed.

"Mr. Lowden!" He shook the old man. "Mr. Lowden—you sick?"

Zeb raised his head and looked at the boy and managed a smile.

"Guess I'm jest tired. . . ."

Jimmy settled back, relieved.

Zeb reached for the canteen and took a long sip of water.

"Mrs. Sutter says she'll get somebody to take your place soon—"

"No need," the old man said. "I'm all right up here. Sun doesn't bother me like it does the others. I'm dried up enough, most likely. And I don't need much food."

The boy squirmed a little and looked over the parapet. "Joe will be coming back with help from Socorro soon, won't he?"

Zeb looked away and closed his eyes. "Yes," he said, through a constriction in his throat.

"Boy, I can't wait to see those troopers," the boy said. He settled back next to Zeb, his eyes shining. "I'll sound the call when they come. Charge! I'll stand up right here, so they can see me, and they'll charge those savages, sabers flashing in the sun. Won't they, Mr. Lowden? Just like the stories my paw used to tell when his company chased the Damnyankees." He turned to look at the old man. "That's the way it was, wasn't it, Mr. Lowden?"

"Yeah," Zeb said. "That's the way it was, Jimmy—sabers flashing in the sun. . . ."

The sound of a hammer striking steel suddenly clanged against the afternoon stillness.

Zeb's mind had been wandering. He jerked his head up now, turning toward the sound, his eyes filling with a sudden anxiety.

"What's that?"

Jimmy crawled swiftly toward the opposite parapet and looked down into the street.

Zeb gripped his rifle. "Jimmy?"

The boy turned his head. "Aw, it's nothing. Just someone in the blacksmith shop, using Big Mike's hammer."

Zeb relaxed. The boy crawled back to him.

"Play something," the old man said. "You've got to practice—for when the troopers come. . . ."

THE KID stood with his hands spread apart, the chain linking his wrists lying across the heavy anvil. The gun in his right hand was tilted toward Ben, who gripped the five-pound hammer in his fist as he steadied the cold chisel in the center of the chain with his left.

"If you're thinking of missing with that, Sarge—*don't!*"

The Kid's voice was level, but his eyes were deadly. The rifle he had brought with him lay at his feet. Selby watched from a few feet away.

Ben raised the hammer, brought it down hard on the head of the chisel. It jumped under the impact, leaving a deep indentation on the chain link under it. Ben raised the hammer again, steadied the chisel, and this time the chain parted.

The Kid straightened, stretching his arms with the satisfaction of a man glad to be free. Two small lengths of chain dangled from his wrists.

He picked up the rifle, holding it in his left hand, and looked at Selby.

"You can go now, Doc."

Selby said, unbelieving: "You leaving?"

The Kid nodded. "Soon as it gets dark." He turned to Ben. "You gonna try to stop me, Sarge?"

Ben shook his head.

The Kid took a backward step toward the street, paused. "Look, Sarge," he said. "I just want you to know how it was. We rode into Spanish Wells to look you up, maybe ask for a handout. We were broke, drifting. What happened in that bank was a mistake." He shrugged. "Like Hank said, nothing ever seemed to go right for us."

"You're making another mistake right now," Ben said. "Two men tried getting out of here on fast horses. If they couldn't—"

"Horses make noise, Sarge," the Kid interrupted. "I don't intend to."

"You plan to *walk* out?"

"A canteen of water, this rifle and shells—that's all I'll need." The Kid's eyes held a reckless glint. "Those Apaches will be on the lookout for riders. I figger I'll get through all right."

Selby said: "Wait a minute, Kid. You can't just

leave like this." Faint anger edged his voice. "You and Ben are the only two able-bodied men here. Those women up there on the roofs—you can't run out on them—"

"You're wrong, Doc," the Kid said. "What happened here ain't my doing. I don't owe them anything."

Selby stiffened. "What about me, Kid? I picked you up out there, made him—" he glanced at Ben— "take you here."

The Kid eyed the older man for a moment. "All right, Doc. I figger I owe you for that. Come with me. I'll get you out."

Selby picked up his bag. "Go to hell!" he said wearily. He walked past the Kid into the street.

The Kid turned, his eyes narrowed, a frown making a V above them. "Doc!" The old man turned to look back. "Why did you horn in out there—stop the sarge?"

"You looked like one of my sons," Selby said. "I guess I was just an old sentimental fool."

He walked off, his shoulders stiff.

The Kid watched him for a long moment. "Crazy old man," he muttered. He turned to Ben. "Look, Sarge—you and me, we could make it out of here."

Ben shook his head. "Go ahead, Kid. I won't stop you."

The Kid sneered. "All right, Sarge—you be the big hero!" He shoved the pistol into his holster and started to back toward the street. "I'll think about you when I get to Tampico."

"Not me, Kid." Ben's voice was grim. "Won't be me you'll remember, but the men lying sick in that room—the tired, frightened women up on those roofs, the children. They'll haunt you, Kid—until you die!"

"Sorry, Sarge. I'll take my chances with the hauntings!"

Ben watched him stride away down the quiet, empty street. A gust of wind flapped the canvas sign just above the Kid. He glanced up at it, but did not break his stride.

XVII

THE SHADOWS began to steal down from the hostile hills, dark purple in color, filling the gullies and crevices and softening the harsh land. The wind off the plain strengthened, moving among the cactus and yucca that dotted the slopes, rustling through the silvery sage. On the lip of the gullies, the bright green leaves of the manzanita danced and twisted as though coming alive with the setting sun.

The three warriors slipped noiselessly down from the high ridge behind the town—lean, sinewy, war-painted, clad only in breech clouts and armed with bows and arrow and a hunting knife.

From way up on the rocky slope, they paused to survey the quiet town below. They had heard of Major Sutter's command before they had slipped across the border. They had seen the uniformed soldiers on the roof tops, firing at the patrols that had tried to raid within.

A thousand soldiers, the reports had stated—exiles from a lost cause. But Tall Bear was getting impatient. They were running low on food, and they needed horses and guns. Taking the town would be a major victory for Tall Bear.

But a frontal assault on a town held by disciplined soldiers could turn out to be disastrous.

Yet for some time now the rebel Apache chief had felt there was something strange about the quiet village. For days now it had appeared largely deserted. And the rifle fire from the roof tops had scarcely been that of trained troopers.

Was it a trap?

Tall Bear had to know. Time was running out on him; any day now Mexican *Federales* could be expected.

The warriors moved again, crouched low, keeping to the gully that slanted across the ridge. The leader, tall and graceful in his movements, was Tall Bear's younger brother, Running Horse.

They moved across the face of the ridge like lizards in a crevice. Midway down the slope Running Horse held up a cautioning hand. His companions halted.

Slowly Running Horse eased his head above the lip of the gully.

The town lay closer below him. He turned and motioned for the others to join him.

A thousand yards below them, a soldier was seated on a box set by the corner of a building, facing the ridge. His face was shadowed by his forage cap. A rifle lay ready across his knees.

The warrior next to Running Horse made a gesture toward the guard below, then reached back for his sheath knife. Running Horse shook his head and pointed toward the sun.

"It'll be dark soon," he said in Apache. "We'll wait."

His companions nodded. They settled back behind the rocks to wait with savage, disciplined patience.

THERE WERE two old men in Mecca. Zeb Lowden was on the roof midway down the street. The man dozing on the box by the corner of the building was Ross Howard. He was shorter than Zeb, and heavier; his forage cap covered a bald head fringed with white hair.

He was in his early sixties, a man with long memories and a short future. He had come there, like many of the others, with his son and his family. There had not been much left of the old homestead after the war, and even less after his wife died.

He had not wanted to be alone during the few years remaining to him. His son was one of the men probably dying in the hotel hospital ward.

Ross was not a man to speculate on the ironies or disappointments of life; he had learned to live from day to day, taking his small pleasures with gratitude.

Now he dozed on the box, his rifle across his knees. In the beginning he had been alert, bright-eyed. He was a passable shot, and he had been acutely aware of the possibilities of a sneak attack down that rocky slope.

But three days and nights of high tension and little sleep had taken its toll of him, as it had of the others. He was tired, very tired, and with the fatigue came a lessening of the desire to survive.

He was tipped back, staring at the hills but not really seeing anything. Something made a sound behind him, but it took a while for it to register. Then he straightened quickly, whipping the rifle around.

Ben raised a hand in a forestalling gesture; he smiled at the frightened look in the old man's eyes.

"Darn it!" Ross snorted. "You shouldn't creep up on a man like that! Came near pluggin' you!" He settled back, breathing easier, but still discomfitted. "You walk just like one of them savages."

"If it had been one of them," Ben said quietly, "you'd be dead now."

"I can take care of myself," the old man snapped.

Ben shrugged. "How long have you been without sleep?"

"Don't need sleep," Ross replied. His voice was still testy; he didn't like being frightened. "Cat nap every now and then. . . ."

The old corncob in his mouth jerked up and down as he talked.

Ben shifted his rifle to his left hand and reached into his pocket for a small tin of tobacco. He held it out to the old man.

"Picked it up in the store," he said.

The old man took the tobacco and slipped it into his shirt. "Thanks, son. But I don't use it." He took the corncob from between his stubby, yellowed teeth and looked at it. "I never light it. Jest an old habit. I like to feel it in my mouth."

He wiped the pipe stem on his pants leg and stuck the pipe back in his mouth. His pale eyes had an old man's knowing smile.

"You get old like me, son, and all you have left are yore habits."

Ben answered without a smile: "Hope I get as old as you, Pop."

"Name's Ross," the other said.

Ben grinned. "Ben Rollins."

"You come to join up with the major?"

"Sort of," Ben answered. He was looking toward the rocky ridge, watching the shadows thicken, blurring the rocks and gullies and brush on the slope.

"See anything out there?"

"Nope." Ross turned to follow Ben's gaze. "But they're up there all right. I can *feel* them!"

Ben placed a hand on the old man's shoulder. "You go on back to the hotel, catch a few winks. I'll stand your watch."

"Don't need a rest," the old man insisted. "Don't do anything but sit." He took the pipe from his mouth and spat on the ground. "You want to do something, you go give Mrs. Sutter a rest; she needs it." He looked toward the hotel. "Fine woman. The major never appreciated her." He shook his head admiringly. "Wasn't for her, we'd all be dead now!"

"Her idea—putting uniforms on the women?"

The old man nodded. "Took over right after the major died." He paused, considering. "She arrived here a year ago; came to join the major. Never understood why. He treated her like—well, nobody knows why she stayed with him as long as she did. But she had enough, finally. She was about to leave—all packed an' ready to go she was—when the major took sick. So she stayed and right after that the 'Paches showed up. . . ."

He reached down for his canteen and took a small sip of water.

"You know the major?"

"He was my company commander," Ben replied.

"How well you know him?"

Ben shrugged. "I was a sergeant. Enlisted men don't socialize with officers."

"Just as well," the old man said. He spat on the ground between his feet.

"I heard stories," Ben said. He looked up the street to the sign hanging between the buildings. "Home of the Fifth Cavalry. Did Major Sutter really expect to form a Confederate state here?"

"Jest stories," the old man said. "Nobody who came down here took him seriously. Guess it disappointed him. But it looked like a good place to settle—close enough to Texas to make a run into Socorro or El Paso for what we needed and still not have to have any truck with them blasted Northern carpetbaggers!"

"What about the Mexican government?"

Ross shrugged. "Guess most of us figgered we'd become Mexican citizens, if we had to. This place was abandoned when we got here. We did a lot of fixing up—"

Ben looked off. He could see some fields, the beans dying for lack of watering.

"Yeah," he agreed. "I guess a man could make a life for himself here."

"Or die!" the old man said. He took in a deep breath, then made an impatient gesture toward the hotel. "You go on, Ben; go help Mrs. Sutter. She can't keep the rest of the women going much longer."

Ben nodded. "All right," he said. "But I'll be back to spell you before dark. . . ."

XVIII

LAURIE SUTTER sat on the side of her bed, resting her head on her arms on the bedside table. She was very tired. This was the room she had shared with Calvin Sutter, a stranger she had met and married while a young girl in Virginia; a cavalry officer just out of Virginia Military Institute.

In the years before the war, she never really got to know him. He was cold, reserved in his courting, and he kept his distance as a husband. He was a man imbued with some inner need for glory that did not include paying attention to a wife. Yet there was some flaw in him that prevented his acceptance by other men as well. For he had been put in command of a Virginia company, a full colonel, only to be reduced to the rank of major later. There was a reason, but he never spoke of it, and Laurie never found out why.

Not that she cared about his military career. She had wanted a husband and found herself to all intents and purposes a war widow. He had written to her only twice during the long war years, and only her insistent writing to the War Department finally provided assurance that her husband was still alive.

He had come to Mecca without her. What had prompted him finally to write to her, to ask her to join him, she did not know. Some need of his, perhaps, or perhaps some subtle form of cruelty. . . .

She had come to Mecca with high hopes. A year of living there had killed them. Not the town. Although born and bred in bayou and Spanish moss country, she fell in love with the desert—the soft dry nights, the empty, compelling vistas, the sense of inner peace it gave her.

And she had come to know that the desert was not as barren as first appeared, not as hostile. Little things lived there; small flowers bloomed at the first rains, tiny flowers that provided startling splotches of color against the sere background.

Down around the creek, cottonwoods grew; birds sang in the branches, perched on the cacti; bees buzzed around the purple flowering cactus pear.

These things she had come to know, to love.

But of Calvin Sutter she learned nothing. He had wanted her there, but she found only an unbreachable wall between them when she came. She sensed, at the end, the inner cruelty of the man, growing older, disappointed, self-exiled and with fading hopes. Even the men he had lured there were not interested in his dreams of empire, of a Confederate state in Mexico.

It was ironic, she thought, that he who had once told her he wanted to die in some battle, at the head of his command—it was unthinkable that he should have died, finally, in a dark back room, unshaven, feverish, stripped of military glamor.

If she had ever loved him, the emotion had long since been forgotten. But she had wanted to be at his side in those final hours, and even this he had denied her.

The chimes roused her—the clear notes of the clock she had brought with her. It had been her mother's, made by some French clockmaker of delicately painted china, the round face held between the loving hands of flanking brass angels.

Four o'clock.

She had not meant to rest that long. She felt an immediate sense of guilt, remembering she should have relieved Ross Howard, changed the watch on the roof.

She picked up her rifle lying across the foot of her bed and went downstairs to the lobby.

THE KID was seated on the sofa, his booted feet propped on top of the long, low table in front of him. He was eating from a can.

He looked up as Laurie paused at the foot of the stairs.

"Hey!" he said good-naturedly. "Doesn't anybody eat around here?"

"You seem to be doing well enough," Laurie said.

"Beans! Found 'em in a store down the street—had to rip the boards off the door." He grinned.

"Don't mind, do you, ma'am? I haven't had a decent meal since I left Socorro."

"I'm sorry for you," Laurie said coldly. She turned away, but the Kid came across the lobby and cut her off before she reached the outside door.

"I bother you, Mrs. Sutter?"

"Why should you?" She was impatient, too beaten down to be friendly.

The Kid held up his hands, showing her the short length of chain dangling from each cuffed wrist.

"I'm an escaped convict," he sneered. "For all you know, I might be a murderer!"

"You prize yourself too highly," she said.

He looked hard at her, not quite understanding. Then, wanting to break through her cold reserve: "I'm getting out of here, ma'am!"

She gave him a faint smile. "Good luck."

She started to leave again, but the Kid reached out and pulled her around to him.

"Ain't you gonna ask me to stay?"

"Why?"

He didn't have an answer to that. He stood a moment, a confused small boy. Then, angrily: "I came here to join up with your husband, Mrs. Sutter. Me an' Hank—that's what we started out for—"

"Hank?"

"Hank Johnson. Me an' him served with the

Fifth Cav, ma'am—under your husband. The sarge, too."

She frowned. "I don't know what you're talking about—I don't think it much matters."

"Me an' Hank, ma'am—the sarge was after us!"

"Mr. Rollins?"

"Yeah—Ben. Sounds more comfortable calling him the sarge. Made life miserable for us most of the time—me, Hank, Brazos and the Deacon. But he was one of us, too. Texas Fifth Cav like the major, ma'am."

She waited, somehow knowing that this boy had to get something out of his system, sensing that in some vague way he felt impelled to explain something to her.

"We rode into the sarge's town 'cause he would remember us. Weren't many of the old company left." The Kid's lips twisted wryly. "Heck, ma'am, we didn't know it was his wife Brazos killed when we robbed the bank. Was an accident, anyhow. It just kinda happened."

He took a deep breath as Laurie didn't say anything.

"That's why me an' Hank headed this way afterward. We were looking forward to a reunion with the old outfit."

"They're in there," Laurie said, nodding toward the closed door, "those who are still alive."

The Kid shrugged. "Yeah. Nothing I can do for them, ma'am." He eyed her. "No point in my staying, is there, if I can't do anything for them?"

"No," she said. Her voice was flat, with no condemnation in it.

"I'll be leaving tonight, soon's it gets full dark." He walked past her to the door, then looked back.

"If I run across anybody, I'll send help."

She nodded, drained of emotion, not reacting, not caring. "Do that."

She didn't move after he left. She stood by the desk, slumped against it, staring with unseeing eyes at nothing at all.

Emma, coming down the stairs, went to her, faint alarm in her eyes.

"Laurie—you sick?"

Laurie managed a smile. "Just tired, Emma."

She turned as Ben Rollins came striding in through the back door. He carried a rifle in his left hand, a box of shells in the other.

He crossed to the two women.

"I checked the women on the roof and the old man down the street, Ross Howard. Everything's quiet so far." He held up the box of shells. "Had this in my saddle bag. I figure we might need it."

Laurie nodded. "I passed out the last of the ammunition this morning. But I don't think a few more shells will make much difference, if they come at us in force."

"They've held off this long," Ben said. "Maybe they'll get tired and ride away."

She looked him in the eye, "You believe that?"

"No," he said. He smiled. She was a beautiful woman, despite the fatigue that put little lines around her eyes and mouth; a strong woman.

"I understand it was your idea, putting uniforms on the women, deploying them on the roofs?"

She shrugged. "One of the few things I learned from my husband."

She turned to the older woman. "We still have some coffee, Emma?"

"In the kitchen."

Laurie motioned to Ben. "Join me?"

They went into the kitchen behind the desk. It was a small, cluttered room with a table and some chairs. The pot sat on a wood stove that exuded some heat.

Ben leaned back in his chair as she poured.

"We've never seen more than patrols," she said, "six or seven of them at a time. At first we thought it was only a small Apache raiding party. We assumed if we could hold out for a few days, they'd go away."

She settled in the chair across from Ben.

"The boy you came here with—your prisoner. You know he's freed himself?"

Ben nodded.

"You don't care?"

"Not any more."

She took a sip of coffee, studying him for the first time, feeling a faint interest in the big man. "He called you Sarge."

Ben grinned. "I guess I made an impression on him."

"Not a good one," she said, smiling with him. Then: "You must have known my husband. . . ."

"I saluted him a few times," Ben said dryly.

"Then you knew Calvin about as well as I." She looked away, not wanting Ben to see her eyes.

"Why did you come here?"

"I've asked myself that many times," she said.

Ben finished his coffee.

"What do you plan to do—if you get out of this?"

"Go back to Virginia," she said. "And you—what will you be doing?"

His voice was short. "I have no plans."

"That boy—the one you call the Kid—he told me your wife was killed—"

"Sue?" Ben stood up, cutting the conversation short. "Get some rest, Mrs. Sutter. I'll make the rounds."

"I tried," she said. "I can't sleep."

"Then try again!"

He walked off, and she watched him, piqued and a little discomfitted.

XIX

THE SUN dipped down behind the distant ridges, and the shadows came out, stealing silently across the land. A coolness more imagined than real rode with the shadows, and the hawks came down from the cliffs, gliding low over the gullied earth.

The Apaches stirred.

Running Horse crept up to the lip of the arroyo and studied the town below.

The corner of the building facing the ridge was deep in shadow, but he could see that the soldier was still there, his rifle propped up against the building next to him. He did not seem to have moved since Running Horse had spotted him earlier in the afternoon.

It was a good five hundred yards straight down—too long a shot for a rifle, out of the question for an arrow.

The soldier seemed to be dozing. The Apache's coal black eyes moved along the building line. He could see nothing move, but this was not unusual; he had seen nothing move in that town for days.

The soldier stretched and turned as a man appeared in the street and waved to him. Running Horse watched all this with patient interest. The man who had waved to the soldier was not in uniform, but he, too, was armed with a rifle.

Running Horse watched the man cross the street and go out of sight into a building. . . .

He waited until the soldier directly below settled back on his box. Then he turned and motioned to his companions.

They slithered down the crack in the side of the slope, angling toward the town below.

INSIDE THE hotel, Emma turned as the door behind her opened and Doctor Selby came out. He was rumpled and red-eyed, his motions deliberate.

He closed the door behind him, smiled briefly at the woman slumped in the chair beside it and walked into the lobby to stand by the window.

Outside, it was getting dark.

Laurie called to him from the kitchen. He walked to her and sank down in the chair vacated by Ben.

Laurie brought him a cup of coffee.

He drank slowly, slumped back in the chair. "When did it happen?"

"Just over two weeks ago," Laurie said. "We buried ten people in one night." She closed her eyes. "That's when Mrs. Devereaux and I decided to quarantine the sick, keep everyone else away."

Selby nodded slowly. "You did a good job. There's a bunch of very sick men in there. But I think the worst is over."

"The women will be glad to hear that."

Selby looked past her into the lobby. "The boy

with the bugle," he said slowly, "where is he?"

"Up on the roof." Then, catching something behind Selby's seemingly idle question, Laurie asked: "Why?"

"Mary Dickenson's boy."

Laurie nodded.

"Mary was my sister." Selby was quiet for a moment. "Mrs. Devereaux told me Mary and her husband, Tobias, were among the first to die."

He stared into his cup. "I hadn't seen my sister in ten years. I was coming here to live with them."

"I should have remembered," Laurie sympathized. "Mary did mention you were coming—"

She turned quickly as Ben came into the lobby and turned into the kitchen.

"How are things in sick bay, Doc?"

"Better than I expected." Selby stood up. "I think I'll catch a few winks on the sofa out there."

Ben said: "Maybe you've got some ideas, Doc. A whole town coming down with typhoid—what could have caused it?"

Selby shrugged. "Some day we'll know more about it," he said, "and how to prevent it." He started to leave the kitchen, but turned as a thought occurred to him.

"It does puzzle me, Mrs. Sutter. You have any idea how it started?"

Laurie's gaze went to the wall clock in the lobby. "Him," she said bitterly. "All I know is people began to get sick right after he arrived in Mecca."

Ben frowned. “Who?”

She got to her feet, still clutching her coffee cup, and went into the lobby to stand beside the window. Ben gave Selby a glance; they joined her at the window.

“Who?” Ben repeated.

“That man out there,” Laurie said, “the one who came out of the saloon when you rode into town.”

Selby looked across the street to the saloon, a professional interest momentarily displacing the fatigue in his eyes.

“The scarecrow with the whiskey bottle?”

She nodded. “His name’s Smith. That’s all anyone knows about him.”

The long shadows from the hills behind Mecca had replaced the blazing brightness of the day. The saloon door was closed; an air of desolation seemed to envelop it.

Laurie turned to look at the wall clock. There was a trace of fear in her eyes.

Almost as though on cue, the sound of someone playing a mouth organ came from the saloon. The music it gave forth was weird, sad, depressing.

Ben and Selby exchanged glances.

“He started playing that the day we buried Tom Starbright,” Laurie said. “He came to the gravesite, but he kept to himself, watching; he was not one of us. Just a spectator, like a man who had seen this happen before. Then he went back into the saloon and played that thing, that music. Every day about this time he starts to play."

"He stays in the saloon by himself?" Ben asked.

Laurie nodded. "He took over the place after Tom died. But he was no kin of Tom's. He came to Mecca alone, a sickly-looking man driving a broken down wagon. Tom Starbright took pity on him; he took him in, gave him a job as a swamper."

Doctor Selby sighed. "Tom Starbright was the first to get sick, wasn't he?"

Laurie nodded. "Then the men who frequented the saloon. Later, their wives. That was when we took precautions."

Selby was staring out of the window. The music coming from the saloon had a bittersweet melody; it was the wail of a lost soul.

Laurie's voice was brittle. "Maybe there's a medical explanation for it, Doctor. But all I know is that it all started in there—in that saloon. And it started immediately after that man Smith came to town."

Ben said quietly: "Doesn't he ever come out?"

Laurie turned to him, her eyes hard. "No," she said. "I told him I'd kill him if he did!"

THE KID came out on the deserted street, a canteen slung across his shoulder, a rifle in his hand. The shadows were thickening in the alleys, graying the land beyond. A bright star winked, a beacon in the eastern sky; it would be time to go soon.

The sound of the sad harmonica emerging from the saloon drew his attention. *A drink for the road?*

The solid door behind the batwings was closed. He banged on it a couple of times, but the man inside either did not hear him or did not want to.

The Kid pushed the door open. It creaked dismally on its seldom used hinges. The harmonica stopped.

The Kid paused just inside, his eyes adjusting slowly to the gloom.

"Hey!" he called. "You got yoreself a customer."

The bar was empty. Dust, sand and a cloying air of desolation had settled in every corner; the few chairs and tables seemed to creak with ghostly memories. The bar mirror was fogged; cobwebs hung their gossamer designs in the corners.

The Kid suppressed a shiver. He *needed* a drink now!

There were some empty bottles on the dusty counter, a half-dozen glasses. One or two of them still held some whiskey. The Kid crossed to the bar, placed his rifle and canteen on the counter and went behind it, selecting a bottle from the few remaining on the back shelf. He came back around the bar, uncorking the bottle, and picked up one of the empty glasses. He wiped the glass rim casually with his sleeve, poured a generous slug of whiskey—

He turned quickly, slopping some of the liquor, as he heard the back door open.

"Hi!" the Kid said. "Guess you didn't hear me."

Smith stood in the doorway just beyond the bar, eying the Kid with sardonic amusement.

The Kid motioned with the bottle. "Join me, mister?"

Smith shook his head.

The Kid shrugged. "Mind if I do?"

"Go right ahead," Smith said. He looked slowly around the room. "Ain't my place—ain't my liquor."

The Kid's hand was clenched around his glass. He frowned. "Owner died?"

Smith eyed him solemnly. "Everybody's gonna die." He held up his mouth organ. "Mind if I play?"

The Kid grinned. "If it's something cheerful, like 'Johnny Reb'—"

"All the same to me," Smith said.

Johnny started to raise the glass to his lips. "Well, cheers."

Selby's harsh voice stopped him. *"Wait!"*

The Kid turned to the door, his left hand reaching for his rifle.

"Come on in, Sarge, Doc." His voice was hard. "Only night spot in town—"

Selby walked quietly to him and slapped the whiskey glass from his hand.

"Leave this whiskey alone!" Selby snapped. "And get out of here!"

The Kid swung his rifle up, eying Ben, who had stopped by the door, then turning his attention to Selby.

"Doc—yo're crazy! I ain't yore patient—"

"You will be," Selby said harshly. "Mine, or someone else's, if you drink out of any of these glasses!"

The one-armed doctor turned to face Smith in the back doorway. "That's right, isn't it, Smith?"

Smith slowly brought the mouth organ to his lips, took a breath—

"Isn't it?" Selby's voice was sharp.

The Kid said roughly: "What are you getting at, Doc?"

Ben Rollins moved into the room. "He's trying to keep you from getting sick, like those men in the hotel."

The Kid stiffened. "Typhoid? In a whiskey glass?"

Selby nodded. "From him," indicating Smith, "to you." He turned to Smith, who eyed him with tortured bitterness.

"It's happened before, hasn't it, Smith?"

Smith's voice was remote. "Happened?"

"Wherever you go, there's a typhoid epidemic."

Smith's eyes lighted up with a deep inner torment. "Leave me alone!"

Selby pressed him. "It's true, isn't it?"

Smith nodded. "Yes." The admission was forced out of him. "Why?" He sought for the answer in Selby's face, in Ben's. He asked out of a helpless anger what no one had ever been able to answer. "Why me?"

He came out of the shadows to stand by the corner of the bar, and instinctively the Kid took a backward step, watching him.

"A pariah," he said, "not wanted anywhere. I've been run out of a dozen towns, stoned, threatened, feared." His tortured gaze went from Selby to the Kid to Ben. "Why? It's not my fault, not my doing! A thousand times I've asked to die, to get sick, to catch typhoid, like the others. A thousand times I've prayed—"

He walked past Selby along the bar and stopped in front of the Kid. He was quiet for a moment, facing the men. Then turning, in one quick sweep he sent the bottles and glasses crashing to the floor.

He put his face down on his arms on the bar, his shoulders convulsed with a terrible grief.

"These people were good to me," he cried. "I didn't want it to happen here—not here—"

The Kid picked up his canteen, slung it across his shoulder and walked to the door. He turned and smiled at Ben and Selby.

"Thanks," he said.

Ben waved coldly. "I hope you make it, Kid."

• • •

ROSS HOWARD, dozing on his sentry box, never heard them. He opened his eyes only when the sharp blade entered his side, ranging upward under his ribs. He gasped, tried to turn. His corncob, suddenly dyed red with blood, slipped from his mouth as he slumped forward into the street.

Running Horse stepped back and wiped the blade of his knife on the old man's forage cap. He picked up Howard's rifle, waved. His two companions came around the building corner, moving like shadows.

Running Horse waited by the corner of the building, his savage gaze ranging the roof line. The warriors slipped past him, one on each side of that deserted street, moving uptown.

Ahead of them, Laurie stepped out of the hotel alley and started to walk toward Howard. Strands of yellow hair carelessly tucked up showed under her military cap.

The Apaches melted swiftly into darkened doorways just ahead of her. Running Horse, beginning to move up the street behind them, spotted her a split-second too late. He ducked back around a corner of the building.

Laurie froze as she saw Howard's body slumped at the far end of the street. She screamed, then turned and started to run back toward the hotel.

The Apache closest to her broke out of the

darkened doorway. He caught up to her before she reached the hotel. His left arm snaked around her neck from behind, jerking her to a stop. His knife hand rose—

Ben and the Kid broke out of the saloon at the same time. Laurie was just in front of them. She twisted away from the Apache and fell to her knees just as Ben fired, his bullet smashing the warrior's knife hand.

The Apache turned and started to run back down the street. The Kid's shot killed him.

Ben ran to Laurie. She was crying hysterically. He helped her to her feet, and she turned to him, shuddering. He held her close.

"It's all right, Laurie," he said; "it's all right."

The Kid was moving down the street, eyes alert. He saw movement in the doorway a few yards to his left and he spun around just as the other Apache charged him, knife in hand.

The Kid fired once, the bullet going cleanly through the Apache, but not stopping him. He jammed the rifle butt up into the Apache's face; then, as the warrior fell, he smashed his skull.

"Close," the Kid muttered. He turned to look back to Ben.

Ben had Laurie's rifle in his hand; he and Laurie were coming toward him.

The Kid said: "Keep yore eyes peeled, Sarge. Might be more of them."

They moved slowly down the street, stopping by

the old man's body. Behind them the "soldiers" of Mecca, the tired, beaten women with rifles they hardly knew how to use, began to straggle out of doorways.

Laurie was staring down at Howard. "I was coming to relieve him," she said. There was despair in her voice, an aching regret. "He shouldn't have died like this."

Ben was eying the darkening slope beyond. Beside him the Kid muttered: "Must have been a small scouting party. Two or three at most—"

Ben took a quick step away from them and fired at a shadow moving out on the slope. It was a good two hundred yards, and Running Horse was moving fast. Ben saw his bullet kick up dirt ahead of the Apache; then the warrior dipped out of sight in a gully.

Ben stared bleakly at the darkening ridge. The Kid shook his head.

"Too bad he got away, Sarge."

Laurie looked at them, shaken.

"Why?"

Ben turned and motioned to the women clustered in the street behind them. Up on the roof, Zeb Lowden and the boy with the bugle were plainly visible.

Ben's voice was grim. "The masquerade's over, Laurie!"

XX

THE APACHE war camp was just over the ridge from Mecca. There were no women there, no children, no tepees. A bunch of Indian ponies stood tethered to a long hoping rope. A few cooking fires burned, their smoke lifting against the darkening sky.

Like all reports of Apache outbreaks, the stories were exaggerated. Tall Bear's war party numbered less than forty braves. And they were getting restless.

Tall Bear squatted by one of the fires, aimlessly tracing a pattern in the sand at his feet. He was a lean, muscular man with an old knife scar down the side of his left cheek. He was listening with little attention to one of his warriors.

"We have wasted enough time here," the brave said. He was angry. "Like old women, we have waited, unable to make up our minds." He slammed a twig into the fire. "I did not leave the reservation for this, Tall Bear!"

Tall Bear held up a hand. "Running Horse will be back soon. We shall hear what he has to say. Then we'll decide."

The warrior settled back on his heels. "Maybe we have waited too long," he muttered. "One of our patrols has spotted Mexican troopers camped south of here." He shook his head. "If they should come this way—"

He paused as a rider came into camp, waving a rifle and yelling. Tall Bear turned. Running Horse slid off his horse and ran to him. He began to talk with savage, excited gestures.

The warriors came to cluster around Tall Bear and listened. "I saw them!" Running Horse said. "Squaws with rifles—tired old women, dressed like soldiers. The man I killed was an old man. There was a boy on the roof, with a bugle."

Tall Bear shook his head. It was hard to believe. He had been held at bay by a handful of women!

But Running Horse was insistent. "It is what I saw. There are no soldiers in the village. Only those men we chased into town this morning, and one of them has only one arm."

He stood tall, waving toward the unseen village. "Only two men, my brother—and a handful of women!"

Tall Bear got to his feet. "Come," he said. "We will see."

THE LONG DAY was ending as Ben shoveled the last spadeful of earth on old Howard's grave.

Laurie and the Kid watched him, flanked by the women of the town. Only Zeb and Jimmy, the little bugler, were not present.

The shadows were thick in the small back lot where other graves, unmarked, made little mounds.

“We buried the others here,” Laurie said, “at night. It was all part of the masquerade, Ben.” She was silent for a moment, listening to the stir of the wind. “But there’s no need to hide the truth now.”

The Kid moved restlessly. “Well,” he said, “guess I’ll be going.” But his voice was not convincing.

Ben ignored him. He dropped the shovel and walked to Laurie and looked off.

“It’ll be dark in a few minutes,” he said. “If they come, they’ll come in the morning—”

The rifle shot shattered the evening stillness. It came from the roof where Zeb was standing watch.

Ben grabbed his rifle and made a run for the street. Zeb was standing at the edge of the roof, reloading, when Ben reached him. Jimmy was by his side, his eyes wide. He pointed toward the hills.

Two riders were coming down the long slope. One of them carried a war lance in his left hand.

Behind them, outlined against the still pale sky behind the hill, the rest of the war party made a savage backdrop. They were mounted, unmoving, watching Tall Bear and his brother as they approached the village.

Laurie and the Kid came to stand beside Ben.

“That must be Tall Bear,” the Kid muttered, “the one with the lance.” He glanced at Ben. “Think they want to powwow, Sarge?”

Ben shook his head.

They watched as Tall Bear and his brother pulled up in front of town. The Apache chief sat astride his pony, in plain view of the men on the roof, eying the village with the fierce gaze of a barbaric conqueror who knows he can take the town whenever he wills.

Zeb started to raise his rifle. Ben stayed his hand. "They're not coming in," he said. "Not now."

Tall Bear slowly raised his lance and drove it into the ground at his pony's feet. He stood for a long moment, defying them to shoot. Then, with fierce arrogance, he turned his back to them, and he and his brother rode back up the slope to join the others on the ridge.

They made a silhouette against the dying day; then they turned away, dipping out of sight.

Laurie's gaze was pulled to the lance impaled in front of them. A small wind ruffled the war ribbons.

"What does it mean?"

"A challenge," Ben said. "They'll be coming back when that lance casts its first shadow in the morning sun."

The Kid rubbed the stock of his rifle. "Gives us a few hours, anyway."

Ben looked at him, frowning.

The Kid grinned self-consciously. "Well, I never really wanted to go to Tampico, Sarge."

He turned to the small boy standing beside Zeb and took the bugle from his hands.

"Here," he said, "let me show you how to use this." He raised the bugle to his lips, turned to Ben.

"How about a little 'Johnny Reb,' Sarge?"

Ben grinned. "Whatever you say, Kid."

XXI

THEY CLUSTERED around Ben later, in the hotel lobby—the women and Zeb and Selby's nephew, the boy with the bugle. The Kid watched from a position by the door.

"It's a lot to ask," Ben said. "I know what you've already been through. But it's the only chance we have."

The women stood silent, too tired to question him.

"They'll be confident," Ben went on. "They know now there are no soldiers in Mecca."

Laurie said: "What do you want us to do?"

"We'll make our stand in here, all of us! The door will be barred; we'll pile all the furniture we can against it. Same with the back door, the windows. Emma, Zeb and about half of you will be in the lobby, the others on the roof. Stay down, out of sight. The Kid and I will handle it. If everything goes right, we'll give Tall Bear the surprise of his life."

The Kid said: "We'll need all the dynamite in town."

Laurie nodded. "There's at least a case of it in the store. Tom Starbright took some before he died; wanted to do some blasting up in the hills. There were some rumors of Mexican silver mines up there—"

“We’ll need coal oil, too,” Ben said, “and boxes of sand.”

Laurie was puzzled. “Sand?”

Ben glanced at the wall clock. “We’ve got eight or nine hours before sunup to get ready.” He turned to the women in the lobby.

“Let’s give them a run for their money!”

SMITH slowly opened the saloon door and stood in the darkness, watching the two men dig a hole in the middle of the street. A wagon was drawn up beside them; Laurie sat holding the reins.

“That’s deep enough,” Ben said to the Kid. “Get the case.”

The Kid hauled a full case of dynamite out of the wagon bed and handed it to Ben, who eased it down into the shallow hole.

“Now for the detonator,” Ben said grimly.

Laurie handed the Kid a tightly bound bundle of dynamite. The Kid watched as Ben shoveled earth over the case, burying it. Then he went down on his hands and knees, scraped earth away from the case, propped the bundle of dynamite on it and pushed earth over it. He left only the top of the bundle poking up into the street.

Ben looked up to the hotel roof. “Think you can see it from up there, Kid?”

The Kid grinned. “I can’t miss it.”

He looked off down the street. “Like you said,

Sarge, they'll be riding straight in without a worry in the world. This should shake them up a bit."

Ben said: "I'll be up there on the veranda, looking down. Those who get through this will be my worry."

"And mine," Laurie said. "I'm staying with you, Ben."

Ben shrugged. "Now let's get those sandboxes loaded!"

Smith watched them drive away. He stared at the small object sticking up in the middle of the street, barely visible now, easily overlooked.

After a long moment he turned and went back into the saloon. He did not close the heavy door.

A candle burned in a holder on the bar top. Smith shuffled to the storeroom behind it and found the dynamite Tom had bought before he died. He picked up the half-dozen sticks, bound them together with some cord, and came back to the bar. Fumbling under the counter, he came up with Tom's sawed-off shotgun. He broke open the barrel, stuffed a load of buckshot into firing position and carefully laid it down beside the dynamite.

He moved slowly, odd thoughts whirling around in his head. Once he paused and looked off, as though listening to something. He shrugged and mumbled to himself.

He pulled a table out to the center of the room, in line with the door. He set the dynamite bundle on it, the shotgun beside it. The candle guttered softly as he pulled a chair from a stack along the wall and dragged it to the table.

He sank into it, facing the door. It was a long time to sunrise. He dropped his arms on the table in front of him and slowly lowered his head on them.

THE SUN poked its red rim above the horizon as daylight rode swiftly across the land, pushing the long shadows before it.

Tall Bear's lance stood imbedded in the earth, a signpost for the warriors riding slowly down from the ridge. They were in no hurry.

Up on the hotel roof, the Kid waited, crouched behind the parapet. He was alone.

The women were inside the hotel, waiting. There was nothing more they could do.

Ben was on the veranda with Laurie, crouched out of sight. Several boxes of kerosene-soaked sand lay at their feet.

Across the street, Smith came out to greet the sun. He stood in the doorway, facing the far end of the street. There was a strange peace in his haunted eyes.

Tall Bear pulled up beside the lance and eyed the quiet, seemingly deserted town. Running Horse pointed to the figure of Smith in the saloon doorway. Tall Bear nodded. He reached down, pulled the lance free.

With a savage, ringing yell he kicked his heels into his pony's flanks.

The Kid waited until the charging Apaches were almost abreast of the hotel; then he stood up, sighting carefully on the exposed tip of the dynamite bundle. He would have time for only one shot. . . .

The earth beneath the Apaches seemed to gout upward as he fired. The explosion shattered windows up and down the street; it knocked the Kid backward on the roof.

Smoke and dust billowed over Mecca; the sign strung across the street tore loose and trailed down the front of the hotel.

Tall Bear, riding just ahead of his command, escaped the blast. It had knocked his horse off its feet, flinging him to the ground, but otherwise he was unhurt.

He staggered to his feet, looking dazedly around. Fully half of his warriors were dead, lying crumpled beside the bodies of their ponies. The others were milling around aimlessly.

Tall Bear shouted a harsh command. A few of them heard him and swung to join him.

Three of them spotted Smith in front of the saloon. The gaunt man had been flung back against the building side; he was getting to his feet when an arrow slammed into his chest. He staggered back into the saloon, reaching for the shotgun on the table.

The three braves dismounted at a run, knives drawn, and followed him inside.

The shotgun blast was drowned by the heavier explosion of the dynamite charge. The violence of the explosion ripped the batwings from their hinges. . . .

Tall Bear and his remaining warriors charged the hotel. Ben and Laurie stood up and tilted burning, oil-soaked sand down on them.

The braves scattered. Tall Bear stumbled, patches of burning sand clinging to him. He tried to reach his horse. Ben killed him with a single rifle shot.

Up on the roof, the Kid had recovered. He worked his rifle with deadly efficiency.

The few Apaches remaining turned and rode wildly out of town!

Ben stood up on the veranda and watched the smoke drift slowly across the roof tops. The saloon across the street was a shambles.

Smith, he thought with detached concern, had found his peace.

Beside him, Laurie stared; her face was dirt-streaked and taut. Ben turned. "It's over, Laurie. What's left of them won't be back."

Reaction set in, and she started to cry. He reached out and pulled the cap from her head, tossed it down into the street, ran his fingers through her golden hair.

"Let's go home," he said quietly.

She looked up at him. “Home?”

He pointed north. “Back to Texas—where we belong.”

The Kid poked his head over the roof above them and looked down. He started to say something, then thought better of it.

The sarge was human after all, he decided.

THE WAGONS stood lined up in front of Mecca, ready to head north. They were loaded with the sick, the women and the children and whatever of personal belongings they had managed to collect.

The Mexican troopers stood by, silent and respectful. Colonel Medares rode alongside Ben and Laurie in the lead wagon.

“We will escort you as far as Socorro,” he said. Then, firmly: “I have your word you will not come back?”

Ben nodded.

The colonel saluted and rode back to his men. They broke into two companies, one of them riding ahead, the other falling back behind the wagons.

The Kid rode up as Ben started to roll. The handcuffs were still on his wrists.

“You sure it’ll be all right, Sarge?”

“Far as I’m concerned,” Ben said, “you’ve done your time.”

The Kid grinned. “Thanks, Sarge.” He looked

down the line to Selby's wagon. Young Jimmy was on the seat beside him.

"Guess I'll be settling down. Doc's only got one hand; I figger he'll need assistance. And the boy needs some help with the bugle."

Laurie looked back once toward Mecca, slowly fading behind them. She was not sorry to leave.

She turned, snuggling up against Ben. "Yes," she said softly. "Let's go home, Ben."

Peter B. Germano was born the oldest of six children in New Bedford, Massachusetts. During the Great Depression, he had to go to work before completing high school. It left him with a powerful drive to continue his formal education later in life, finally earning a Master's degree from Loyola University in Los Angeles in 1970. He sold his first Western story to A.A. Wyn's Ace Publishing magazine group when he was twenty years old. In the same issue of *Sure-Fire Western* (1/39) Germano had two stories, one by Peter Germano and the other by Barry Cord. He came to prefer the Barry Cord name for his Western fiction. When the Second World War came, he joined the U.S. Marine Corps. Following the war he would be called back to active duty, again as a combat correspondent, during the Korean conflict. In 1948 Germano began publishing a series of Western novels, either as Barry Cord or **James/Jim Kane,** stories notable for their complex plots while the scenes themselves are simply set, with a minimum of description and quick character sketches employed to establish a wide assortment of very different personalities. The pacing, which often seems swift due to the adept use of a parallel plot structure (narrating a story from several different viewpoints), is combined in these novels with atmospheric descriptions of weather and terrain. *Dry Range* (1955), *The Sagebrush Kid* (1954), *The Iron Trail Killers* (1960), and *Trouble in Peaceful Valley* (1968) are among his best Westerns. "The great southwest . . ." Germano wrote in 1982, "this is the country, and these are the people that gripped my imagination . . . and this is what I have been writing about for forty years. And until I die I shall remain the little New England boy who fell in love with the 'West,' and as a man had the opportunity to see it and live in it."

Center Point Publishing
600 Brooks Road • PO Box 1
Thorndike ME 04986-0001 USA

(207) 568-3717

US & Canada:
1 800 929-9108
www.centerpointlargeprint.com